THE
UNFADING

BY
OLIVIA STOGNER

The Unfading

ISBN 978-0-9828151-0-6

Library of Congress Control Number: 2010930570

Unfading Press
Burlington, NC 2010
theunfadingbook.com

Cover Design and Text Format by Kimberly Martin
Cover Illustration by Olivia Stogner
Author Photograph by Suzie Stogner

Acknowledgments

This book has been long in the making and I have many to thank. My Mom and Dad, Rodema and Bob, have always encouraged my creativity and supported me with such love. My brother, William, has spent countless hours helping me to go from manuscript to book. His interest and effort motivated me to keep going and helped me through the details of publishing. My sister, Suzie, lives her life uniquely and encourages me to do the same. Her compassion has been influential in my life and in my writing.

My extended family has always been a part of my life. I am thankful for the legacy of reading, story telling, and creativity that has been passed to me and for having the Wright connections. The kids also inspire me and help me stay imaginative: Erin, Clay, Katelyn, Carson, Cameron, Riley and Kyleigh. I hope Makayla and Tyus will enjoy this one day, along with the Diaz girls, the Johnson boys, the little Stones and Emma. I also hope Emma B. and Madi will love this one day too.

Amy provided the roots for Ara and is my sister by choice. She and her family always make me feel at home. Laura provided Ara's new wings and is my traveling companion from China to Colombia. Both have taught me a great deal about friendship. A collection of early manuscript readers were gracious with their time and gave needed encouragement and critiques: Mom, Dr. Kristen Pond, Cousin Steve, Cousin

Sara, Aunt Elizabeth, Kari Ann, Amy, and Laura. More readers and supporters have also come along. I appreciate each of you. Those ideas, words of encouragement, and questions became the stepping stones I needed to keep moving.

Sally Buckner provided editing services. Susan Dalton and Elizabeth Sharpe gave help in proofreading on subsequent drafts. For this I am thankful. Mom, Suzie, and Aunt Anna read the proof copies. They helped with a few more corrections and gave some eleventh hour encouragement. Kimberly Martin has been gracious with her time also.

There were many good teachers along the way who set me off on the right path. Southern Wesleyan University and UNC-Greensboro also allowed me to keep plying my trade and meet new people. I am also thankful for the support of my students and colleagues at Alamance Community College. The English department has become a second home. My church family also continues to provide a community of support. The Voice of the Martyrs, Open Doors, and World Vision keep me connected to the world and to those who need a voice to speak for them.

Momotaj, my little girl in Bangladesh, brightens my life with her life and letters. I am grateful to Compassion International for allowing me to be a part of her life and their work in releasing children from poverty. Syshma, my little girl in Nepal, is also a bright light. Tiny Hands is an amazing organization and I am thankful for them. I am also thankful for Not for Sale and for those involved with the organization who encouraged my writing. The fight to end slavery has informed even my fiction and Fair Trade shopping has revolutionized my life.

Traveling has opened many doors and I am thankful for those who have opened doors to me and made me feel at home in South Dakota, Jamaica, Croatia, Germany, China, Colombia, Massachusetts, and California.

Those who have made the music, which accompanied my writing, especially in these last rounds of editing, are a appreciated: Delirious, Tom Conlon, Shaun Groves, Jars of Clay, Coldplay, U2, Bob Dylan, Switchfoot, Seabird, Andrew Osenga, Ben Harper, Josh Ritter, and Joan Baez, among others, and especially Tom and Shaun because I can call you friends.

George MacDonald, C. S. Lewis, Madeleine L'Engle, and J. R. R. Tolkien have been wonderfully real in my life because of their writings. So have many other authors. This is my way of beginning to put into practice some of the things they have been teaching me. I plan to keep reading and learning.

Over time, I began to feel that this story wanted to be told. I am thankful for God's blessings of imagination, time, and community that allowed me the opportunity to give the story a life of its own. Some things are unfading, even now, if we will seek them.

Part 1

Carina

On a clear evening the waters lapped softly, slowly carrying a small vessel. It was a carved craft, something like a walnut shell missing only a quarter of the upper covering, or perhaps rather like a cradle, rockers needless in the waters. Only it was, by necessity, much larger than these and more slender a craft, meant for one down a wild, winding river. It was carved of a solid tree, dark wood, bearing emblems. A carved stream traced its way around the craft and produced flowers and fruits. It ran its way around the cover of the craft. There, at the top of the arch, a single jeweled tear drop hung suspended on a circlet of silver. This jewel was poised as if it would in a moment fall and yet it was quite firmly held by a small silver clasp. Just below this drop, a small girl sat and looked up at the jewel and the bright white wisps of stars that shone through it. Now you may think a child should have been frightened to be left alone at night in a boat, even one so curious as this. But you see, she did not think she was alone, and that is precisely because she was not.

In the deep dark just before the light, the diminutive ship and its even smaller passenger landed on a sandy bank in a little town. The child, sensing the ceasing of the caressing motion of the water, sat up and began not so much to cry as to stir and mumble a few words as if to wonder why the ride had ceased.

Soon a fisherman, coming to begin his day, saw the boat and pulled it farther ashore. Discovering its cargo, he picked up the little girl who smiled just a little. Her bright green eyes stared at him through dark lashes and the dark wisps of curls falling in her face. But there was no fear in those eyes. The fisherman smiled too, a slow, full smile and the light of the fading stars caught in his own blue eyes. He looked around for a moment, up the river, down the river, and finally to the stars still in the sky. A puzzled look crossed his face and the child grinned; she reached out her small hand for his. He carried the little girl home, and his wife met them at the door. They loved the child from that moment, and they called her Carina.

The Fading

From the beginning Calder and his wife, Eldoris, as Carina's parents were called, knew she was special, special as all children are, because they are children. Still, they could not help but wonder where she came from and why and how. Of course here and now inquiries would have been made in a different fashion. But as Calder and his wife had no way of knowing where the child came from or to whom she belonged, they did their best to seek it out and, in the meantime they did their best to care for her as their own. So try as they did, they could find no more of a beginning to her story.

It was true that when Carina came to them she babbled something very much like a language, but not one they understood. Eldoris, especially, had listened intently and had even written down some of Carina's words. She thought it was something that Carina should not lose and yet she could not crack the code, as it were, of this language. It was a mystery and had something of antiquity to it; it had something of the music of moving waters. It was a strange clue. But then Carina was so quickly learning the language spoken around her, as children often do, that her first language quite unintentionally, but with lack of something better to do, faded away. Eldoris, with a sigh, finally let it go. She was happy to have Carina.

Calder, on the other hand, did not put so much stock into strange ways of speech and dreams of far off lands. Loving them both as he did, he let it pass with a smile and shaking of the head, and in the course of time as Carina grew, the strangeness of her coming rather seemed to fade away too.

In this way, Carina grew. She went fishing and swimming with her father. She took easily to the waters. At first Calder took her to a stony stream beyond their home. There he held her in the waters and she splashed with joy. When she learned to swim, he took her to the Blythe. On market days she helped him sell fish. On the way home he would give her the shiny coins to carry to her mother. He watched over her and wondered at her.

She helped her mother plant melons, carrots, lettuce, radishes, and tomatoes, in neat rows and due seasons. There were rows and bowers of flowers in their little garden too. There was a trellis with yellow roses and a purple clematis vine grew along the fence and gate. A bevy of other types of growing things found themselves at home in Eldoris' garden. Carina also learned her mother's songs and stories. They were often acted out. Eldoris made her dolls and she dressed them in the scraps from her own dresses.

Evenings were times together. There was always a good meal and sometimes a guest or two or three. There was time for singing songs and telling stories. Then there were quiet times, too, when Calder and Eldoris would hold Carina until she fell asleep and then her father would carry her to bed.

There were also times filled with laughter. Calder liked to laugh and he liked best to make Carina and Eldoris laugh with him.

Then, sometimes they all took walks down by the river and up the streams away from the sounds of the village. They all enjoyed the quiet, or rather the living sounds, of the forest, different from those of the village. But of course, you will want to know what village.

Yes, the town of Keldalee, on the river Blythe, near the seat of the Ruling House, had there been one sitting, in the land of Kelwynden. Now you may feel quite confused with these names, but this happens when you travel. You may find that in Kelwynden your name is quite unheard of. So you must learn these as best you can. At any rate, it was a lovely town with plenty of space. There were a few clusters of homes near the river, where Carina lived. Her own was a little white cottage, with a red tiled roof, and situated on the hill facing the waters. A few more homes were further up the river and then there were some inland facing the hills. These were made in similar styles, but varied in hues. There was a town square, with gardens where people often gathered. Around the square the houses were taller, more slender, and, perhaps, more uniform. But it was still a very pleasant square and ivy flourished along the walls, windows, balconies, and lanes. There were several other houses a little space from the town center and, beyond, facing the hills, more fields and a few scattered houses. There were a few neighboring towns, upstream and, some, further inland, but beyond these the roads were little used. For Keldalee was the last village before the river emptied into the bay on its way further out to sea. After Keldalee there were wild woods and marshes. Most of the travel came and went by way of the waters.

Eldress Altea

When Carina grew a little older, she went for a few hours each morning and nearly every afternoon to one of the larger houses in the village. It was an old stone building, crawling with vines. It also served as the school. She could easily head out of her front door and cross the village square. Or, as she often preferred, she could leave by the back door and take the route through the forest. There she could cross Winding Brook and listen to the many birds that called overhead. It was a sort of school, but perhaps not what you may think of school. If the children were not mindful, they were not simply met with a waving of the finger and "tut, tut." They were sent home to their parents, until they cared to listen. But not many children were sent home because here they wanted to listen to the stories being told.

There Carina learned stories about so many things. There was the ancient history of Kelwynden. She learned this through poetry, ballads, and paintings as well. She also learned stories of far away places and far away peoples and people quite different from those she knew. There were people who lived in the sea, not like mermaids with fins, but people who could swim wonderfully and breathe in the water.

They lived beyond any reckoning and were said to know much of the old stories. Then there were those said to have lovely wings, who could fly. They had forest homes, but had long ago been scattered about. Grownups, when acting quite grown up, sometimes called them, "myths and tales from long ago." They said, "Well, perhaps there were, but of course there aren't any now. You don't see them now, do you?"

And of course that was not a very good argument for the children. So it hardly kept them away. Then, of course, most of the parents did not keep the children away either. Sometimes it was because they really believed, or wanted to believe, or because they recognized in the school's leader, they called her Eldress, a certain knowledge and wisdom; or because it simply was somewhere to send the children for a good bit of the day. Although not everyone wholeheartedly believed Eldress Altea's stories, there were few who would or could reckon with her wisdom or her kindness.

The Eldress was often known to take a volume or two from the library and sweep up the stairs in her long skirts and cape, out onto the balcony. There she let the wind play havoc with her hair and dress, but she sheltered the leaves of the pages. And when she came back down, she told the stories with all the glory of the wind. Some still said it was all superstition. But as the Eldress Altea told Carina, leaning over her with a smile and whisper, "Just because it becomes a legend, it does not make it untrue."

Elias

When Carina first began her studies with Altea, Eldoris or Calder would walk her to school and come for her when it was time to go home. One afternoon she had been allowed to stay in the town square playing with some of the children. They had been jumping rope and telling stories. Some of the others decided to go walking into the forest upriver and Carina was not yet allowed to go so far without one of her parents or Altea. So she decided to see if Altea was at home, after all. As she approached the house she saw a figure sitting on Altea's front porch. He wore a dark cloak and had a bundle across his back. His gray shirt was embroidered about the open neck in a simple fashion, like the ones her father wore, but his boots were of a taller sort and worn but well made. He wore a sword as well and looked much traveled. Still, he smiled at Carina and there was such light in his smile and his face.

"Sir," she asked, "are you waiting for someone?"

"Yes, I am. Today I hoped to see the Eldress Altea. She is an old friend of mine. Only she seems not to be at home."

"Oh, I hoped to see her too. She told me she may be making a journey today. If she is gone she will likely not be back until night. If you are a friend of the Eldress I am sure you are a friend of my family too. Won't you come and wait with us instead?"

"That is very kind, my child. Thank you and tell me who do you belong to?"

"I belong to the sea," she said teasingly and laughed.

"Yes, I see." He grinned playing along, "and your father and mother are Calder and Eldoris are they not?"

"Yes, they are. Do you know them too?"

"Yes child, I do. I am Elias, an old friend."

"Oh, Elias, I know you. I have heard your name before. Where have you been so long?"

"Has it been so long? I feel as though I am always among my friends in Keldalee, although they do not always see me."

"Oh, is it like a pleasant story then, one which stays in my heart to help me when I think of it? And it isn't there, and then suddenly it is there when really it has been there all along?"

"It is something very like that. And I have many friends in many places." Then he paused, still smiling, and continued, "As you seem to like the sea and stories, how would you like to hear a story of the people of the sea? I can tell it as we walk?"

"Yes, please. I would like that very much. Only Eldress says sometimes I ask so many questions."

"It is not always a fault to ask questions, child. Seeking can be good."

"Yes, but I think finding is better," she again laughed and he smiled as she took his hand.

He told her the story as they walked along the path together. When he had finished a short story he asked, "Did you know that when the children of the sea laugh it sounds like music?"

"Really? Do they make bubbles too? Like I do when I laugh under the water?"

"Yes. A child's laugh may break into hundreds of tiny bubbles, which all go skipping up to the surface, and when this happens you know it is a special child."

"Have you seen such a child?"

"Oh yes. I have seen several. I know them too."

"I wish I could know them."

"Well, it may yet come true. It does not often happen and, yet, sometimes, it comes to pass. I know of a little girl who once lived on land who went for a ride across the sea on the back of a great lady of the waters."

"Really? How did it happen? Where did she go?"

"Her parents were in trouble. They were in trouble for helping others and the child was not safe. They called for help and it came from the sea. Do you suppose they were sad to let their little one go?"

"Yes, very, if they were good parents like mine. Then again, if they let her go, they must have been very good parents."

"How do you know, child?"

"They loved her enough to let her go."

So Elias spent the day with Calder, Eldoris, and Carina. They told many stories and went fishing and then made their dinner on the shore by the firelight.

"Elias, my friend," Calder spoke, "It is good to see you have returned to us."

"Yes," Eldoris added, "We had so hoped you would soon be able to meet our Carina. I can hardly believe it has already been three years now since she came to us. Such a gift she is. Can you believe it? I almost feel as if she had been sent to us. I suppose that is silly."

"Oh, no, not silly at all," Elias added, looking at Carina. He smiled, "There are many things we do not see when we are not looking for them and many things which yet find us."

"You speak like the Eldress," Eldoris laughed. "I am so glad you have come that Carina might meet you."

"But I have seen him before," Carina suddenly announced.

"Where have you seen him, my star?" Calder questioned with a wink.

"I do not remember where, but I know I have seen him before," and she smiled at them all and ran toward the river, splashing joyfully and calling them to come and join her.

The Forgetting

Calder and Eldoris had told Carina, as soon as they perceived she would understand, of her coming. However, they told her in the simplest terms and tried to make little of the mystery. As she grew, she found there was something in the sound of the water, a long ago memory, a voice. Carina loved to go boating with her father and feel that she could sit upon the water and learn its ways, its voice. Sometimes, as she did, strange words would come to her mind. She could not explain from where, or even why. Yet, she longed to know. For as much as she loved her mother and father and her life in Keldalee, a question, a longing, lingered.

One evening, after Altea's lessons were over, Carina wandered away, slowly meandering at first, but later stepping lithely through grass and heather to the hills just beyond the village and before the wild woods. There she stopped by a babbling brook arrested with its murmuring.

"It seems as though it really is trying to speak," she thought. "How delightful," she whispered aloud. "But of course that's foolish, really," she reconsidered and reprimanded herself.

But then it seemed the brook countered, "Is it now? Come and listen, come and listen. Look and see, look and see. Ask and find, ask and find. Come and listen, come and listen."

As she sat by the stream, she closed her eyes and began to try to follow its sounds. Of course to most, the language of a babbling brook is just that, babble, and what Carina did not realize was that several of the other children had followed her and finally caught up with her.

Lethia, a girl a few years older than Carina, began to laugh and mimic Carina's song. Which, of course, was not only cruel and foolish, but it broke the spell and brought Carina all too quickly back into the world of Lethia. Carina, confused, stood up and, looking around, saw several of the others following Lethia.

Lethia, narrowing her eyes and spending a few minutes arranging her hair and smoothing her ruffled and frilled dress, finally looked up and asked, "What were you babbling about? Don't you even know our language? You must be a slow learner and Altea seems to think so highly of you. But just look at you now. Not anything, not a drop of a royal line at all, such as my family. Well, what does one expect? Come on ladies let's leave this babbler and her brook."

Carina looked down and saw her own simple dress. She had thought it pretty when her mother had made it. It was a pink empire waist gown with open half sleeves and it fell about her legs in soft waves. Now she only saw how plain it seemed. Then she looked at her bare feet and legs splashed with water and dirt, and, lastly, she noticed the tresses of her long hair falling down again, despite the bit of shiny ribbon purchased in town. Her father had been correct. Her mother's own hand crafted bands held her hair better.

As the distorted laughter of Lethia and the other girls echoed over the hill, a few tears slid down Carina's face and dropped down into the brook.

Carina's walk home was slow. However, the next morning she put away the shiny ribbon and she thanked her mother for working so hard on her new pink dress. Calder looked on and smiled.

It was not many days later when Carina came to the Eldress.

"Where am I from, really?"

Altea began, "Dear child, where you come from I am not yet sure, but that you have a purpose I know. You mustn't be afraid of those who would mock you for being yourself. You must not begrudge them either. It may be that they, not knowing who they are, are jealous of you."

"But Lethia, the others, they know where they come from. Their families are here. They are strong, old, wealthy families. Lethia says they are of ancient royal lines."

Altea smiled, "Ah, but Lethia can be a bit forgetful of the things she wants to forget."

"Still, she knows where she's from. Of course she knows who she is."

"Are you sure? Is knowing your history the same as knowing who it is that you are becoming?"

Carina sat in silence. She knew Altea was right, but, all the same, it was not that pleasant sort of right.

"Well then, come sit by me and let me tell you a story. How about something of the people of the waters, so nearly forgotten they are or the winged ones, or, yes, I know something of the ancient kingdoms? There was once a bright and fair place on the banks of a river leading to the sea. The people of this kingdom were in many ways like us, except they had been blessed with a spring of fresh water, which poured from a place deep and close to the source. It was a bright, ethereal city with many rooms and houses with turrets and towers glistening, from which the flowers and gardens seemed to pour as water. There was no gate because there was no wall around the city. It was still early in the world and the winged ones, living in the forests, and those of the sea, and those on land all lived together well." Altea paused and Carina waited.

"This spring was no ordinary spring. It had been given by The Sceop, the great shaper and maker of all things, the One Great Giver, The Source." Altea smiled and paused, "You know, any spring is a thing of wonder, for precious water comes from it. But this spring was even more wonderful. It was a well of truth. A sick child could come and drink and be well. A blind man could wash in it and see. One with a bitter heart could listen to its song and learn to forgive. Of course people sometimes tried to bottle it and take it with them or sell it, and it was water just the same, with the effects of any water. Once in a while someone would come and prick his finger and stick it in the water and it would only bleed. The water was alive and it knew not only the body, but the spirit.

But as it was such a spring, most were content to share its use
and to give to those who needed.

"But there was one who was jealous. He thought if he
could control the spring the people would be at his mercy. He
also had some power, but it was not the power of creating and
shaping, but of twisting and distorting. The people of the sea,
being even closer to the waters, had tried to warn the others
of such happenings. The ruler of those in the waters spoke
with the appointed king at the giving of the spring. He told
the king that this great gift of life could bring both blessings
and curses and one must be careful in the choosing. For this
sea king was a wise and kind ruler who befriended his neighbors because they cared for the stream and its life and its
Giver. And for an age it was well this way. But in the end a
Twister of Tales came to the kingdom in disguise. He even
told the king that he had come with a great new wisdom. He
said things that were sweet to their ears and so the people
listened. He tricked them into making him the king and he
denied the One Giver. He made them deny the truth of the
One and silenced the telling of his stories. In doing so he also
filled the spring with the filth of his lies and it came to be but
a small dark trickle.

"The truth is that this new king had deceived the people,
spreading lies. He convinced many that he should be made
ruler. But he was of no line of kings and he treated those who
spoke the truth very cruelly, putting them in prison, or
threatening their families. His power was in his lies and he
made them sound sweet, but in the end they turned bitter.

"He built a fortress around the spring and a wall around the city. He allowed only those he wanted to enter the fortress and those were few and far between. At last there was a great battle. Then the followers of the One Giver heard his voice saying go out of the city and to high ground, and so many fled. The enemy thought they were winning until the spring began to grow. It became a torrent and with the sound of the rushing of many waters the fortress was broken, the wall washed away and the great city was flooded, but left clean. No longer could the one spring be found and yet rivulets flowed over the land and far afield.

"Those who believed would continue to seek and to find water, life giving and sweet, though not as it was before and yet in sundry places. But those who doubted could see nothing, or would settle for a small trickle of muddy water running off some roof rather than to seek."

With that Altea ended her tale and Carina sat amazed and wounded.

"Altea, such good cannot end that way, to be wholly snuffed out in evil!"

"Oh child, I am growing old and weary. It is only a tale my own mother told me and you will hear that it isn't true."

"Then is it not true?" Carina asked.

Altea smiled, "Carina, what did I say?"

"You said that I would hear that it was not true, but you did not say that it was not true. You said that the kingdom was flooded, but you did not say it was the end."

"Yes, Carina, you've learned to listen well, like your mother, Eldoris. A bright pupil she was too. You are both much alike in many ways, many good ways. Only I think, my child, you are even closer to waters, their movement, their glare, their murmuring."

Children Grow

For the next several years Carina drank in Altea's stories and Elias' visits. He too told stories and sometimes he came to the school or sat on the greens and told them all wonderful tales. He was always coming and going, and yet Carina often saw his stories in her mind, even as she heard Altea's. There was always joy in his visits and, yet, sometimes a sad something too, like something unfinished and waiting. Carina often wondered about this.

During this time, too, her mother taught her of history and they sang songs as they sewed or baked. They tended the garden and her mother taught her the names of the birds.

Her father taught her to fish with a net, a pole, and a spear. In fact, she could catch the little minnows in the shallows in her hands. Only, when she did this, it was always in play. She laughed as they tickled her fingers and then she let them go.

Her mother's songs and soft care and her father's strong, quiet comfort gave her a shelter better than any roof or walls.

She made flower chains with the other village girls and wove stories as they wove stems. Carina, it seemed, had become a great favorite as something of a novelty. It was not only her story telling in which she acted the parts, but her long dark hair and sea green eyes made her stand apart from the other girls. In spite of Lethia's protests, the others often listened to her stories. Carina, unknowingly, made those stories seem even more real, as if she were a part of the stories herself and they were a part too. But when the telling was over, the others wandered away. For Lethia had sweets and coins for the shops in the square; Carina had only her stories. Carina longed for something lasting; she longed to know who she was. She thought, if she just knew where she had come from, she would understand.

🍂 Once and Again

On a bright spring morning, Carina awoke to the sounds of her mother singing. This was not such a strange thing and certainly not a bad thing. It was the song itself that was unusual. It was beautiful and familiar, but also far away. The song inspired her with much awe and a certain joy mixed with a tingling dread. She asked her mother what it meant. So her mother sang the song,

"Once and again the little ship shall sail
Shall sail once and again
Once and again the sick shall be made well
Made well once and again
Once and again once and again
What happens, happens
Once and again 'til the end
Follow the river down
To find where it will begin
Once and again, once and again

Well, these are at least the words I learned from my mother. But you, Carina, came to me singing the same little tune, but with other words. I don't know what; but I knew then that you were meant to be me mine and so you are. I woke up today and the song was in me."

A few days had passed when Carina, helping her mother in the garden, asked, "Can you tell me anything of those other words I spoke?"

"Carina, have you been thinking much on this?"

"Yes, mother. It seems it won't leave me."

"It seems so long ago," she spoke softly, "and yet but a day since we found you." She stroked Carina's hair and continued, "Well, we shall wait until your father comes home and talk over it more. It is nearly time for dinner. Now come tell me what you have learned from Eldress Altea as we clean ourselves up a bit."

When Calder came home, after a day of fishing, and they had eaten together at the little round table, he and Eldoris went outside to talk. Carina went up to her room. It was half of the attic, as it were, her bed surrounded on two sides by shelves of books. She turned from these to look out of the round window at the moon. She saw her parents walking, and then they paused. Her father took both of her mother's hands in his own. They looked at one another and both nodded and smiled and yet, in the star shine, Carina thought she saw a tear slip down her mother's face and her father's too.

A little while later, Calder and Eldoris entered slowly through the back gate. Calder called to Carina and she came down the steps. He held out his hands to her. "My Star, come here. We have something to speak of." He smiled and Eldoris also reached out to embrace Carina, as she so often did. Yet, Carina felt some heavy thing weighing on them. They gathered around the fire and she waited. Calder again took her hands in his. He took a long breath and then he began. He told her, again, of her coming and everything he remembered of finding her. Then her mother told her of the language she had spoken and how it had rather faded, except for a little book of phrases she had copied, guessing the transcription, and something that had come with Carina. It was a tattered, fading bundle of pages. It was written in other characters, wholly unknown. It looked to be a part of a great, ancient book. These pages had been carefully wrapped and preserved and sent with Carina. Lastly, they showed Carina the little craft. Calder unfastened the tear shaped jewel hanging by its silvery circlet, and he handed it to his daughter.

"Carina, my Star, we never meant to hide this from you. We only wanted to wait until you were ready, and we see now that you more than are. You will have many questions, as I know you to have of a normal day and now so much more. We have few answers, I'm afraid. We ask only that, for now, you complete your training with Eldress Altea and with your mother and that you consider the life you have here. You are full of stories, I know, and while fourteen seems a ripe old age to you, you have many stories to learn still and time for them. What I am saying is only to be careful in the choosing. Do not feel that that you must grow up too quickly, looking for something, you know not what. Give it some time. That is all we ask, and if a day comes when you may find out more, then you will be the more ready for the finding. We love you. You are our own and always will be."

Carina nodded. There were tears in her eyes. Her mother had been holding her hand. Now she touched Carina's long hair and kissed her cheek. Then Calder turned to Carina. For a while he held her as if she were that bonny little girl he had found along the river. She felt overwhelmed that so much should be shown and yet so much remained veiled. She already had so many questions and now even more. She had known that she was not from this village and yet she knew no other home. She had imagined herself as a part of Altea's stories. She had imagined herself as being descended from some high royal line and what it would be like to tell Lethia that she was a real princess. But now she began to wonder, would it not be simpler to just be, to be any one of the other village girls with a plain and lovely life ahead, with few questions that needed answers?

"There is one more thing, my Star. Although Altea knows all, there is no other who knows more than that you were found along the river bank. We thought it just as well. Also, Altea seems to think the pages there are quite rare and old and must belong to some great ancient work. She seems to think it very important, but she will not say exactly why. She says she can not read the language though. It is a strange tongue and quite faded, as you can see, and yet she seems to feel it is quite a legacy for you and one we should keep, perhaps, to ourselves until we know more of what it all means."

Carina went to see Altea who, although she did not know the language of the faded pages, did know of a man who was said to be wise and well versed, and if he could be found, was the most likely to know. Altea could tell that it was an ancient tongue and not one used by the people of this village or her ancestors. She thought it was an ancient script used by the people of the waters, written by those who lived in the sea. She hesitated to tell Carina all of this, but did at last, thinking, somehow, it may be of help.

"The man who is likely to know lives downriver, on a branching of the stream; although, he can be difficult to find. He is an old friend and well versed as well as wise. I think this book has a great role to play."

"But Altea, if I want to find news of my homeland it seems I must go upriver, from where I came."

"It seems," she repeated. "But who is to know from whence you came, little rivulet?"

After this Carina and Altea sat, for a long while, on the little balcony running the length of the back of Altea's home. They looked inland toward the mountains at one end and seaward following the river at the other. They seemed to be at the very joining of sea and land. Finally Carina spoke, "Altea, what must I do?"

"Questions, always questions it is with you and how I do love it. But this time I have no answers to give you. You must follow what way seems right to you. You have a little time yet and I think when it comes to it, you will know which way you must choose."

At this, a great wind blew down from the mountain shaking Altea's cloak with some force and it sent Carina's hair flying loose. The vines stretched from the trellises, like arms reaching out. It floated around them for a moment and then headed out to sea.

Ara's Arrival

It was not long after that when a new student arrived at Altea's doorstep. Her name was Ara. She came in quietly with her shoulders low and her head down a little. But she bowed to the Eldress, and she looked up and smiled at the class. Carina thought she must be nearly her own age, only Ara seemed a little smaller, quite petite really, and her hair was not nearly so dark as Carina's. Rather, she had a head of strawberry golden curls. Carina noticed her slippers, too. They were not of the sort the village girls wore, leather with a buckle. They laced around the ankles with embroidered ribbon and looked to be of rather delicate satin, only worn with walking. Her long crimson cloak also looked fine, but used to the weather. It brushed Carina as she took the seat beside her. Ara pushed it back, but did not remove it. Carina smiled. Ara smiled in return.

A few days later Carina asked her mother if they should not invite Ara and her family to dinner, especially since they had not long been in the village. It was agreed and Altea was to be invited as well.

Carina walked out of class with Ara that day and asked her if she and her family would like to come and have dinner the next evening.

"Oh yes, that would be nice. Only, it's just my father and me you see."

Carina answered, "Well then we'll see you and you father tomorrow evening, and the Eldress will be coming too."

Then Carina went to invite Altea. "It is a shame Elias is not here now," she thought. "I know he would love Ara. But he is always coming and going."

The next evening came and it was a lovely dinner, with everyone around the table: Carina, Ara, and Ara's father Tobin, Calder, Eldoris, and Altea. Such lovely stories and jokes and laughs were heard floating out over the river.

Then Calder asked, "Well, Tobin, what brings you to these parts?"

Tobin and Ara both grew quiet. Then he began, "My wife, dear Airlia, Ara's mother," he added, "passed away, of an illness, just about two years ago. We miss her so still, and my son, he took it hard, as we all did, but we each deal with things in different ways. He is still so young. But he started taking long walks out into the woods and fields. We should have stopped him from going so far, but I knew he was grieving and the walks seemed to help, and I was grieving too. Then, one day, he just disappeared. It was the same day as a large ship left, and so we have tried ever so much to find him. But, at last, the trail has gone rather cold. We've no other family, in these parts at least," and he looked at Ara. Then he smiled, "Well, and it's been hard for my little dove moving so much, and she's held up under it so well. Then I have to stop and work and the…well it's just nice to be in a home again, with such pleasant company. It's not that we mean to give up the search, mind you, but we know no where else to look now." There was a pause, Carina looked at Ara and touched her arm.

Then Calder said slowly, "We're sorry for all of your troubles. I can't imagine, but of course you're welcome here, my friends."

"We enjoy your company so much too, and Ara is such a good friend for Carina. We could not have asked for better," spoke Eldoris. Then she looked at her daughter and wondered what life would have been like, for them all, if Carina had not come. Then she looked at Ara.

After this, Altea gave them a story. She told them of the winged ones in the great forest kingdom and of Vara, the wandering stranger, and her adventures. Carina looked at Ara and could not read the look of wonder and pain mixed in her face. She thought, perhaps, she missed her mother.

By the end of the evening, Calder had asked Tobin if he might be able to help him in his fishing and in some work he was to do in the village repairing one of the houses.

"You see, Tobin, I've just been overwhelmed. Carina and Eldoris are a great help to me, but I suppose I can't have them with me in my work all the day long. It would be a favor to me, if you could help me out."

In this way, the next several months slipped quietly and quickly by as Calder and Tobin worked together and Ara was a frequent visitor to Carina's home and Carina to Ara's. Altea helped Tobin to secure a little cottage of his own, close to the school.

As the girls sat late one night in Carina's little garret room, talking over some of Altea's stories, Ara asked, "Carina, what do you think is your greatest desire?"

Carina told her of her strange coming and of all she knew of the waters. "I should like to know so many things. I suppose my greatest desire is to know who I am and where I come from. I feel I must know. And what is your greatest desire?"

Ara, in turn, told the secret of her mother, Airlia. "You see, even as most don't speak of it now, but my grandmother was one of the winged ones. My mother had hoped and felt that I would be given wings too, even though she herself had not been. Although in this age most would say it is just as well. But I would not mind the stares and taunts, if I could fly. But I have only these strange knots on my back. I hate to think of them, even, except they remind me of my mother's songs and prayers. She longed to fly and she longed to know more of the ways of the winged ones. She told me all she knew from her mother. She told me of her dream to seek out the forest home of her ancestors. I long to fly, it is true, but even more I long for my family to be together. That would be my wish, my brother home, my family all together."

🦋 Changes on the Wind

A lready, Carina had advanced in language studies. Even beyond the library, she searched the corridors of Altea's home and school, for all of the books she could find. Ara's arrival had only driven her more as she searched for anything which might aid Ara in her own studies. The girls compared notes and read by sunlight, moonlight, and candlelight. They told stories by the hour and wandered through the forests and glades. So a year passed with Carina and Ara as the best of friends.

One day, as Carina was searching Altea's library, the El-dress came in. "Carina, child, have you found what you are looking for?"

"I am not sure, Altea. I had thought there should be a book about the Battle of Lockwood Hill, and yet I cannot find it. There are stories which are mentioned, but not wholly here."

"Yes, it is, perhaps, more often that way than what we would like. Carina, you have advanced in your studies now, and you have helped Ara so much and many of the others. I think it is nearing the end of your classroom studies. You will no longer need to sit with the group but of course will be free to continue on your own course. You are fifteen, now, are you not, by your mother's reckoning? You have worked so hard. You are a good scholar and a good child, and now you are growing as well."

So a celebration was planned, like those of old, on the ancient span of green, just across the river and downstream a little. It meant extra work, but Carina insisted it was the only place right for such a party, and her friends agreed. There was to be a moonlight picnic with music and dancing and the telling of tales.

On the eve of the day of Carina's party, a ship stopped in Keldalee. This caused some stir. Ships passing were not so strange. But ships stopping for more than just the usual trading were rare, especially a ship such as this. It was high and grand, gilded and gold, almost royal looking, but very dark. It was carved with intricate shapes and designs, almost a language, but nothing of life. Still, the villagers were elated. Any ship meant new things to trade and news from other places. But these were usually travelers and merchants; no one expected them to stay very long. This ship seemed different from those, grander somehow, as did its captain, Captain Malwell. Those who were there told others, and soon a small crowd had come to see this ship.

Malwell came down the walkway on a dark carpet lowered from the ship by some of his faithful hands. They were in uniforms, dark, crisp, and new. Malwell himself was lavishly attired. It was something of a uniform, but it had a sort of sheen to it, like light reflecting in the fog surrounded by mist, but with a dark sort of glow. Malwell was also covered by medals of gold and bright ribbons, and his cap bore a ring of twisted gold. There was something very stately about the ship, a pretense of power. According to taste, of course, it was not altogether unattractive either, rather like Malwell himself. He was tall, but not too tall, slender, but not too slender, with nothing of roundness in his face. His eyes were so alert, almost piercing, and icy blue.

Carina's party had by now become something of a village affair, a large picnic. Most were celebrating, some were just curious. None were to be turned away as friends and neighbors had come together to help. Malwell, new to the town, walked about listening and nodding and smiling a great deal. He was charming and his manners were impeccable. His sailors were gracious. They helped where they could in carrying and arranging things and then stood back to admire the beauty of the party.

Malwell himself was intrigued by this party, as a revival of long ago traditions and story telling. He was anxious to know its cause, and this was easily remedied. He asked one of the locals about the whereabouts of the honoree of the party. His attentions were directed to a young lady, lovely in pale silvery green that changed colors with movements much like that of water in the low light of lanterns strung around the green to give aid to the lone moon. Her flowing sleeves waved as she animated the telling of some wild tale. All this Malwell saw in a moment without the girl seeing him. Then he whispered something to one of his men, and the man quietly left the party only to return, in other clothing, and slip a little box into Malwell's hand.

The sailor, now disguised as a villager from upriver, approached Carina.

"Good evening fair miss. I do wish you fond congratulations and many happinesses."

"Thank you good sir and have you traveled far this night hearing of our celebration?"

"Indeed I have, and I am finding it well worth it. But I was hoping to hear a story."

"Well, there are many in the telling and to be told this night."

"Ah, but I was hoping to hear a story from you, and particularly, one about those mountains. I had family who lived there many ages ago they say. They used to tell me something about a wonderful spring with magical waters. But I suppose that sounds silly to you."

"Oh not silly at all, it's just that, perhaps, you have your stories confused. You see these mountains are—"

"Perhaps we could walk as you talk and we might see the mountains better if we walk but a little."

In doing so, this sailor was able to distract Carina and take her out of the main crowd, not so far as to be unseen, but rather as to be unreached, at least by most.

Carina began again the story she knew of the mountains.

"The Eldress Altea told me that in ages past, much farther up river, beyond these mountains there was the Summer Palace of the Queen, Lady Adria, and the King, Lord Gresham. For they meet in the valleys below Lockwood Hill. There was later a great battle on that very spot."

But not long into the telling, the man from upriver became restless. He looked about, and then he stopped Carina.

"Oh say, that music is lovely."

"What?" she asked coming out of her story.

"Let's stop the story and have a go at dancing, hey?"

"I thought you wanted to hear a story?"

"Well, yes a story, a story as we dance!"

Carina, perturbed by his lack of interest in the story after all, turned back to the party green. As she did so, he grabbed her arm. "No, let's dance here!" He tried to swing her around.

But she got in one good kick, which sent him limping. Then almost as if on cue, Malwell appeared.

"Unhand the lady, you vile creature!" he yelled. This, as it happened, was already quite unnecessary.

Then as Malwell turned to Carina, the man conveniently slipped away. The commotion had brought a crowd, and Malwell was pronounced a hero, if only for being the first one there. But with things as they were, they soon returned to the party. Malwell approached Carina again, as she stood with her father. He asked Calder's permission to ask Carina if he might be honored with a dance. Calder paused and looked toward Carina for an answer. Something about Malwell seemed too polished. But he had come to her aid, it was a party, and he was her guest. She also saw Lethia watching her. She nodded to her father and curtsied to the captain.

Malwell swept her around the party green so that everyone might see. They were really rather stunning, if only in their contrasts, him in his dark, fading mistiness and Carina in her star-like clarity. When at last they stopped, she felt she was still reeling a little. Then Malwell pulled a black velvet box out of his jacket pocket and handed it to Carina. She thanked him. He nodded, and she concluded she was to open the little box. Inside was a large, shining black pearl. It was set in twisted gold and hanging from a ribbon of intricately patterned black lace. It was lovely, but strange. Even as Carina held it, she felt its weight pulling.

"Shall I tie it for you, Miss?" He asked this smiling, one dark eyebrow raised in question.

For one moment Carina stared at him and into his eyes. She leaned ever so slightly, holding the lace in one hand and he took it. He was just reaching around her neck when he was startled with a push, as some dancers passed a little too closely. The pearl dropped. Then as if waking up, Carina turned and quickly picked the necklace up, placing it in the box and placing the box in the pocket of her bright new sash.

"Oh, how careless of me," she added. "I hope you will excuse me now, Sir. You have been ever so kind, but I am afraid I must be keeping you from other company."

"Not at all, my dear. I know few people here, save my sailors, and I do spend a large amount of time with them, as it is, you see."

"Well, then, I expect you will want to mingle and make other acquaintances, and I dare say you won't have much trouble. As it is, I am quite afraid I have old friends to attend to as well. Do enjoy the party and good evening."

As Carina turned, Ara met her, laughing. She apologized, "Forgive me, dear. I'm afraid Papa and I are not so light on our feet as we should be, and I'm afraid in our last turn we may have stumbled into that man who was talking with you."

"Oh, it's just as well, Ara. In fact I'm glad."

"You are glad we're not good dancers?"

"Oh no, of course not. I mean, well yes, I think I am. Oh shall we walk a bit, and I'll try to explain?"

"Yes, I think you'd better. You know, Carina, since we came here you have been my dearest friend, but with you there is always another story."

Carina and Ara walked off arm in arm, and Carina told her friend of the strange gift and the strange giver.

Malwell watched them go and thought Carina must be showing off, as he would certainly have done, and for that he was rather pleased. Thinking things had gone rather well and feeling he had done enough work for one night, he retired while the party was still going. He returned to the ship to find a sailor in costume, with a bruised leg, awaiting his arrival.

Another Story

The next day Carina went to visit Altea. "Come in child, or perhaps I should no longer call you so, but so it is how you shall always seem to me. And to what do I owe this honor, you who have lately finished your studies with me?"

"Oh Altea, I shall always learn from you. I suppose you would let me stay on and study and help you with the little ones?"

"Yes, if that is what you wish, I should be glad to have you continue here."

"I do not know. You say that I have finished my studies, but there are still so many questions. I have even more now, and there is at least one story which I must know more about. Tell me, again, what else you know of the spring."

"I supposed questions would come. Not all were destroyed in the flood or the battle. Some were helped. But the evil lingered too. It was not as it was intended to be. Eternity in such a world is no great blessing. Their lives were changed. There were some who continued to live long lives, especially those who had tasted little of the dark water of the Twister of Tales, and of course the people of the sea live longer than any, even the winged ones. But still it would have been only misery for them to live forever as things had become. As there were good springs spread across the land, there were others as well. Yet, it is said that those who did not turn with these twistings lived out their lives here only to make a great journey to a place of no more weeping, where no evil may ever go. The land of the Source, the Sceop, past the Arvel Veil. There was also another promise given, that one day, a new spring would be found. It would not be as it was before and yet it would stand as a promise and a sign."

"Then, it is a real place?"

"Of course it is a real place. But that doesn't mean you may simply go there whenever you please. It is not that sort of a real place."

"And the spring, it is real? Then can it still be found?"

"Of course it can be found, child. But as wondrous a thing as a spring is, still more wondrous is its source. Things are not always as they seem, and sometimes it is in searching that we know we are lost, and in being lost and letting go that we are found." Altea sighed. "Perhaps I expect too much of the child," she whispered to herself. Carina did not hear her. "But you have other questions too I see, my child." Altea waited.

"Yes, I don't know how to say it. When the ship arrived, I can't say why, but it held little interest for me. But last night at the party there was a horrible man from up river, and he grabbed my arm to threaten me, and suddenly he was there. Captain Malwell was defending me. Then we danced. It seemed everyone was watching and admiring and…and he danced with no one else. When I left him, he left the party. I don't know what to think, Altea. I feel ashamed at liking the attention, but I did."

"Oh so honest and thoughtful. I suppose it is natural that you should like some attention. But if that is all that you think of yourself, where will it lead when such attention fades? Carina, many gain honor for wrongs and petty things, but is that the sort of fame you would be known by? Would it be better to gain attention for any vice, or silliness, than to go upraised by the fading masses?"

"But then what will not fade? What will last that I may trust? All things seem to fade," Carina murmured with downcast eyes.

"No, no, Carina. You must not think that," and a shiver seemed to run through Altea. Carina sat up again. "Some things do not fade. Rather, they become even more brilliant and wonderful with time." Her voice softened, "There are some things unfading even now, child, if one will seek them."

The Tavern Raven

A few days later, after his initial success at the party, Malwell and his men went to the Tavern Raven. Calder was there as well. He sat quietly off in a dark corner, beyond the dying embers of the fireplace, and as such he was quite nearly invisible. Calder had been troubled and gone to speak to Altea earlier. Then he had spent some time walking in the upper greens before coming back to town. He was on his way home when he had slipped into the then warm tavern to think a bit more. It had been quiet then. Quiet until Malwell and his men came in, and Calder was startled from his musings and broodings by their talk.

Malwell, perhaps a little too taken with his welcome, began to speak to his men of their fine new town. "Of course it will need some fixing up, fellows, and we'll need to get rid of those lingering, ridiculous stories. But that can all be done. I'm quite sure. We wouldn't, after all, want people finding things out or remembering too much, except what I, the Captain, shall do," he laughed.

Calder thought perhaps it was just his drunken state, but then a worse mistake was made.

"Aye Captain, but you did look a sight dancing at the party with that lovely lass, only so foolish a girl. It's a pity she didn't meet you sooner, hey?"

"Well, Captain, there's still time for some learning, I say!" one of the men added.

And they broke into laugher.

Then another of the men added, "She be fair enough, but I wouldn't have her. She kicks too hard. I've still a bruise from her slipper, and I didn't even get my dance in with her or any other before you jumped in to save the day, Captain."

Then they repeated, "Unhand her foul villain!" and laughed again.

Malwell smoothly replied, "But it did work, didn't it? Like a charm, even, I'd say," he added with a wink and a finger laid aside his nose.

"But you realize, men, she's just a child, a pawn in the game. I've bigger plans. I just hope she won't be too in the way. But best not to say too much here my fine fellows. The work is just beginning and we haven't the run of the place, yet that is."

At this, laughter broke out again.

It was too much for Calder. He perhaps should have just walked out and told what he knew. The stories were one thing, but his only child was another. He stood up, shaking off his cloak.

"That's right what you say. You don't have run of the place."

Malwell was visibly shocked by Calder's sudden appearance. For once his shoulders dropped and his smile faded.

"Malwell, I may make exceptions for strangers and perhaps even for drunken talk, but you talk of my child, my star, and I won't let that pass, far from it. You deceived us for your own glory. You put my daughter in danger and disgrace for a little game, and now you openly threaten her? How you can call yourself a captain, even a man...those are titles too good for one like you."

"Now, now Calder, what do you propose, a fight?"

"If that's what it takes to be rid of you."

"And how shall it be, Calder, now?" he asked as his sailors gathered round.

Calder looked at them; there were at least six. Then he lunged at Malwell, knocking him to the floor. The men came at Calder, but Malwell, hearing steps coming, quickly called them back.

Just at that moment the tavern owner returned from the cellar.

"What's going on here? Calder, I've never known you to cause trouble, or be inhospitable to a guest, especially one such as the good Captain here, with his good men and his good business."

"Oh, no sir," broke in Malwell. "No trouble, just a bit of high spirits, and I believe Calder here was just on his way out, home to his lovely wife and darling daughter no doubt?"

Calder nodded, "All right, this time you spoke first. But who you are has become known, and one day others will know too. You'll trip on your own quick tongue and fast feet sooner or later. You'll fall, if you're not pushed first." He said the last phrase looking over Malwell's shoulders at the men behind him.

Calder did go home to his wife and daughter. He told Eldoris of Malwell's treachery at the party and all that he had said concerning Carina. He only told Carina that she should avoid Malwell and his men and that he was not to be trusted. He hated to reveal to her the whole story of how she had been used, especially when the party had been such a crowning moment for her.

After this misadventure Malwell realized that, perhaps, he had not impressed quite everyone, and he certainly did not want Calder spoiling things for him in his new town on the river leading to the bay. Most of the other villagers thought him grand and kept inviting him to visit and to tell his own stories of adventures at sea. Malwell was a talented storyteller. But it was not of the kind that Altea could give merit to.

Altea's Visit

Altea walked up the flowered path and opened the garden gate with her walking stick. Eldoris heard her and knew that if Altea came by way of the woods and back garden entrance, it meant she had taken the long way, to think.

"Ah, Eldoris, you were one of my brightest students, and your Carina has followed in your steps. You learned to question and to believe."

"Eldress, I thank you, and did you come all this way just to pay us gracious compliments?" she asked smiling and turning from her weeding.

"No, I'm afraid not. I've had a visit, a visit from Malwell. He came in and asked to see the library. He said although he knew many things, he was interested in preserving works of great antiquity, and he asked if I had any especially old or unusual books. I took him through the library, the one the children use, and he ranged upstairs and down, looking, but not seeing. Finally, I asked him if I could be of help. I told him I knew several volumes which might do him much improvement. He gave me a wry smile and thanked me, no just the same.

"He even said he was saddened that the greatest teller of tales had not come to hear him, and he had been anxious to meet me and to hear what I would think of his stories. He began to speak such nonsense. He told me that the old stories were not altogether false, but not altogether true, and that he knew what they needed. He knew what we needed. He hoped that I would support him. He seemed to imply that if I did not, I shouldn't like the results."

"Altea, what did you do?"

"I stopped him right there and said I would most assuredly not support his twisting of that which is good. The old stories were intended to leave something lacking that we might have questions and seek out the answers. But he is not that answer, and has shown that truly in his behavior and in his attempts to use the old tales for his own gain."

"And what did he say?"

"He said he was sorry to hear that, and he had hoped we might be able to come to some sort of understanding. He did leave then, Eldoris, but I think not for long. He was angry. He wants glory for sure, and likely he sees Keldalee as a prime location on the river, leading to the bay, the sea, and the islands. But there is something deeper too. He seemed to be looking for something, and most of all, he wants the people not to know the truth."

"Then we shall tell them the truth."

"Yes, we shall, and yet, they can't be made to believe, Eldoris. They must learn to think for themselves. If they do not, I see in this danger for you and Calder and Carina. I wanted you to know what it may mean for you if we stand against this man."

"What do you mean, Altea?"

"I am old and alone. All I have are my lingering days, my stories, and my friends, and I will fight for them. But you are still young and you have a husband and child to think of."

"Altea, surely you must know we would not leave you alone for our own comfort or even safety. You have been a mother to me and grandmother to Carina, and we believe in the stories even as you do, even if we may seem to understand them less. Altea, Calder was never so much for the old stories as I, but he accepted them for my sake. As Carina has grown, something has changed in him. I know he would not want to see a day when one such as Malwell was given control over the people. I suppose this means you have already spoken to him then?"

"Yes, you are still my discerning pupil. He cares greatly for your safety and that of Carina and mine as well," she paused and smiled. "He is a good one, child. He has cared for me as a son would a mother. You have all become my family here." She paused again and then continued, "He would that you, Carina, and I prepare to leave now, but I told him I think it best to wait a little still. Then he wanted to gather the men and wage war, but Malwell has not come just with weapons, but lies. There will be another type of battle too, and I think he has a part to play in it. Still, I am not altogether sure it would be unwise to lay aside some provisions and to gather those who are sure to be with us, and there is the matter of Carina and her legacy that you both must consider. She is no ordinary child."

"Do you think the book and the jewel are really so valuable that they would put her in danger?"

"I do indeed. It was an ancient volume Malwell was searching for, after all. Carina's legacy will put her in danger and give her hope. I had thought that Carina would pursue the study of the old stories and the language of the book by now and find out for herself. But the time may come whether she chooses it or not. The stories will lead her."

"Perhaps, they will have to lead us all," Eldoris agreed with a sigh.

The Great Debate

On the other side of town, farthest from the sound of the water, Malwell and his men were still staying at the Tavern Raven. It was positioned just outside of town and bordered the upper greens and the forest. It was generally an out of the way sort of place, used by travelers from up river and a few regulars. Calder used to like to stop in after a long ramble or work up river, but he and Tobin had not set foot in the place since Calder's meeting with Malwell there. However, many others did, and Malwell had taken to holding informal meetings in the courtyard outside of the tavern.

It had been little more than a month since Malwell's arrival and he had planned another one of these meetings. He stepped up on a table in the courtyard and began to speak to those visiting, "Ah good people, yes, yes you are. You would say no, but I know better and I know you better, and you are some of the best people I have had the pleasure of being able to say so to. I have traveled to many places and places, such places I have seen. But there have been no places with such faces as yours. You need not turn to another; you have only to look in a mirror to see such life and wisdom and such beauty and strength. For you to welcome me and my weary sailors, and then to deign to listen to my tales, it is such an honor, a true honor and humbling, so humbling. What could I possibly do to repay such good people as you?

A voice from the crowd spoke, "Tell us a tale!"

It was followed by others, "Yes, a story! A story, please!"

"Well...if you insist. I suppose you have heard of the kingdoms of long ago? Yes, yes of course you have. You have tried to keep the stories and so well. You know there was a kingdom once with a fountain, a spring. Some claimed that this spring had wonderful, magical, life-giving powers. But others said it had done little good, and so it seemed. Then a new wise ruler came, who would have been the truly best king, as any one could plainly see, for he could make real use of the spring. He could bend it to his will. No other person had even attempted such. He was so brave, this new king, to strike out and do something on his own. But some of the foolish people stood by the old king, and so unfortunately, they thought they still had to follow all of the rules of the old king, and there was a great battle. But just as it seemed victory was on its way, the one who made the spring to begin with caused a flood to destroy them both. Quite foolish, as any sensible person could see. What was the good of it? Destruction, when the new king was building? What was the good of it? None of course, but that he was afraid of the power of the new and real king, as you intelligent beings before me can plainly see.

"Well now, this is the true account, as you good citizens can no doubt give account. Of course it makes more sense to those trained in the ways of wise thinking than the old version you may have heard somewhere or other. I myself have told this story to many a brilliant man and woman and many wise and powerful rulers. They believed me; it is true. But what is more, I have it all written down, in an ancient text, which I intend to translate for you and for the good of us all. You see the old king had laws yes, but also walls and the new king offered new ideas and good ideas. Now tell me, which will you have, the old king or the new?"

The people cheered and clapped, shouting, "another story, another!"

But this was interrupted by Altea, "Now, Captain Malwell, perhaps, as you said, you were saddened that a great story teller such as I had not come to hear you. Well here I am, and I have heard quite enough, and I am prepared to reply, if you are not afraid of the stories of an old, weary woman?"

Malwell had not expected this so soon, but he countered with his charm, "Of course not, dear Eldress, it is your wisdom that had kept the bit of the stories alive for the people until I came to amend them. Please speak what you think you know."

The Eldress began, "Malwell, you may have some skill, I'll admit. But I shall spare you what I think it lies in. Instead I shall tell you not what I think I know, but what I believe and have always said to all of the people here. The stories of old were left to us, with some questions, yes, that we might ask and seek. There is One Great Giver, The Sceop, The True Source, who gives all fountains, and all stories, and we must seek him."

So Altea told the story of the ancient kingdom. She spoke of the good king, who was yet deceived, the treachery of the usurper, the wisdom and aid of the people of the water and the winged ones, and how trouble had entered, but also with it the promise of life still to come.

Then she added, "This is what you have always known, from your own parents and grandparents; just because it becomes a legend does not mean it ceases to be true. Think for yourselves. What is true in your own life? What kind of life would you like to lead? If truth has been scattered, then we must work to find it. It is not an easy task. Think what this will mean when you choose the one you will follow. Think what kind of leader this will be. Is it one who creates, gives, and shapes or one who usurps, takes, and twists?"

After this, such an uproar arose that the debate was effectively ended. From that day forward some agreed, and they stopped listening to Malwell and went to visit Altea. But others were tired of the old stories or had never really believed them. Still others liked Malwell and the flattery he poured upon them. They thought he would bring wealth and high living, such as the new king of the story. Some others believed in the stories and thought, perhaps, Malwell really held them in the book, which he promised to "translate" for them, for they had heard stories of such a great book.

Meanwhile, Carina sat at home with her book and studied over the strange characters. She traced the lines she could see with careful fingers. She closed her eyes and tried to picture them in her mind. She could not begin to unravel their mystery and yet a voice called to her, even so, like the murmuring of a far off stream or the first strains of an old and distant song.

The Village Council

A few days later Malwell called in one of his soldiers. "Nuewell, you have done something well at last. Do you know what is in this stack of old papers which you collected from the magistrate's office in the square?"

"No, Captain."

"There is a copy of the charter for the Village of Keldalee on the Blythe, the ruling seat, of the Great Land of Kelwynden. How splendid. It confirms what of course I already knew, but it confirms. Would you like to know what it says?"

"Yes, Captain, if you would like to tell me."

"This and that, this and that and here we go '…this village having not had a king or queen sitting at the castle of Veradis Kel for many long years, shall be governed by a council. While once the land was ruled by both those of the sea and those of the land, when strife threatened, this combined line was broken long ago in The Battle of Lockwood Hill. It is said that one lingered, descended from the royal line of the first queen, who was of the sea, and who had married one who was of the land. It was said that this ruler would be able to prove the right to rule. If this one comes, the council is to make way for this ruler as are all other councils in the land of Kelwynden. However, anyone who claims this right, without producing this proof, must be punished…Yet, if one comes who is proclaimed ruler, by the will of the people, then the people shall obey this ruler until one of real royalty comes who can claim a higher right.' Now, is not that just lovely?"

Malwell could well be pleased with such a charter. Those who had made it had not envisioned one such as Malwell. Yet, they had made a provision for a ruler, who was not the true ruler. Perhaps they had done this with good intentions. Yet, it was a dangerous thing. For this reason the town leaders and council members had to be careful, and they had kept the council going and never entertained thoughts of another sort of king or queen.

Now, Altea was one of these council members, and Calder was on his way to being one, many agreed. But there were others on the council who had perhaps been sitting too long. They liked the rules, and they liked the sound of their own voices, perhaps too much. Malwell stirred up the people. He curried favor with those on the council saying that what they really needed was a strong king, such as himself, to lead them and further their causes. He would bring what was needed to set things right again and to fulfill what they had long purposed. At the same time, he suggested to those who opposed the council that they were truly weak and failing, and now would be the best time to be rid of them and induct new leaders. Malwell stirred seeds of dissention, discontent, and discord. He played one side against the other, to gain, in the end, what he alone desired. Perhaps this was the skill Altea had spoken of.

Altea thought this over as Calder stopped by the school grounds as the children headed home.

"Greetings, Eldress," he said pushing back the hood of his cloak. "How are the children progressing?" He asked this as he picked up a little boy and swung him around as the child laughed. He sat the child down, "Run on home now, Adric, and study well."

Altea waited and then replied, "As well as can be expected for each. I do enjoy them. I learn so much from them still, and what brings you to the school house today?"

"Well, how was the last council meeting? I wanted to be there, but Tobin and I had some work that needed tending to upriver."

"Yes, Adric's home upstream had some damage in the last rising of the river. I remember. It was kind of you. You are a good man. That was a better use of your time anyway, I think. Malwell has so much pride. He has been allowed to address the council openly. Some protested, but we were overruled." She added this last part with an annoyance which was seldom to be heard in her voice.

"But do you think he would openly proclaim himself king and make war?"

"Oh no. He knows the laws of the land, even if only to subvert them and use them for his own gains. He is hoping to be made king. That would serve him far better. Yet, violence he may well bring. How much he may dare, I do not know. Calder, do you understand what this means?"

"Eldress, I do not understand at all. But I understand that Malwell endangered my daughter and then bragged about it. I understand that he contradicts you at every turn and I will do whatever I must to protect my family and my village. What other choice do I have?"

"What other choice indeed?" Altea looked away. Then she turned back to Calder and smiled in a half sad sort of way. A tear ran down her face. He wrapped a strong arm around her shoulder. "Altea, you are always the one telling us to hope. I will follow your example. Let's have no more tears now."

Back at the Tavern Raven, Malwell sat alone. None would dare disturb him, unless he called. His plans for a new residence were already going ahead, under the vague cover of "village improvement." He had even managed to use some of the council's funds. He studied over these plans. He looked over records of his past travels and, finally, he smiled a little as he looked over a map of the town.

He also knew the myth, as he called it, of the spring and the sundering of a certain ancient book. He was careful, for he knew something of the author of this book that he was not willing to forget. Yet, as he traced his hands around the map, it all rather seemed too easy. It seemed easy, except he had found an obstacle in Altea and those who believed with her. He also had a certain fear of Carina. She seemed to know so much and so little at the same time. It rather unsettled him. He also feared Calder, because Calder had heard the truth and was, Malwell thought, perhaps just reckless enough to do something about it.

 Calder

C alder had heard the truth. He knew that Malwell had to be
stopped. Calder also sat up many nights staring into the
dying embers of a yet live fire and wondering how. He thought
about his wife and his daughter. He thought about his friends
and about the children growing up in the village. Something
seemed to burn in him and he knew. He knew something must
change.

Calder had warned Carina about Malwell, and he was sure
that she was wise enough to understand that Malwell was a
twister of stories rather that a teller of truth. Calder had also
tried to spare his daughter and even his wife from the depths of
Malwell's intent. He knew that Carina had questions of her
own, and she talked of taking a journey upriver to see if she
could find anyone who might know of her origin. So, as difficult
as it was, Calder realized the time had come for Carina to make
plans for a journey. He knew families in several towns upriver,
and he could make arrangements for her to visit them. He
hoped Eldoris might go too, but he doubted it. He knew there
was no changing Altea's mind. Then a thought came to him. He
wrote a request for Carina's safe passage and took it to Altea to
have the council sign. "Calder, it is sad we should even have to

consider such a step," Altea said. "Things like this were never needed before. What made you think of it?"

"You said, for now, Malwell was playing by the letter of the law. I thought on that and thought of this." Then Calder went home and spoke with Eldoris. The next day they told Carina. She could hardly believe her good fortune.

Once, together, they had polished and repaired Carina's little boat. It was with a quiet sort of sadness that they thought again that it would not do for an upriver journey. They searched for another craft. They also gathered food and other such needed supplies. Calder gave Carina fishing line and a small new net that he had been preparing. Lastly, he gave her a spear. He had fashioned it himself working into the night by the light of the stars that had brought Carina to him. He had carved the long oaken shaft to bear the names of her family. His only hope was that she would not need it, other than for spearing fish.

Carina had been excited about her journey, but now something seemed to change. She and Ara had been to visit Altea, and then they had stopped at Ara's cottage for a while. It was a shady little gray stone place, near Altea's. Ara and her father had worked to brighten it with a lovely garden.

As Carina walked home from Ara's, something was strange and strangely missing. There were no children running across her path, nor playing in the town square, nor on the greens on either side of the river. She could not hear laughing or voices. Only the gritting, grating sounds of Malwell's men's boots on the gravel and the click clack of boots on the new walkways resounded. Even the very birds seemed hushed or flown. There was such emptiness in it all. Yet, the people listened to Malwell.

Why? What had once been curiosity in the town's people turned into fascination, and then enchantment. They ceased to seem to even want to know the truth. They seemed to prefer to be spoon fed rotten refuse, rather than to dig for hidden delights. Carina could not understand why. She was suddenly glad she was leaving this village.

 Eldoris

The sight of Carina's own home was a welcome relief. The garden door was open and, through this, she saw her mother get up and begin wiping the table. Then a look crossed her face, a look that Carina had never seen. She was in pain. Days went by and Eldoris grew worse. Altea came and went often, and at last Eldoris was confined to her bed, and no one knew why.

Eldoris was usually up early singing, as she cooked or sewed. She tended her garden and took times for walks, visiting neighbors, and talking with Carina and Ara. Carina had known her mother to rest, but she had never before seen her truly ill.

Ara came and sat with her. Sometimes Ara tended to Eldoris so that Carina might help her father. Tobin was a frequent visitor too. One afternoon, Carina and Ara were sitting together in the garden. Calder was with Eldoris.

"Ara, I am afraid. I am so afraid she is going away from me."

"Carina, some say I lost my mother and yet I know she is with me in a different sort of way. In her words, and songs, and hopes for me—she still is. Beyond that, even, I believe, she still is and I will see her again one day. Eldoris has been so kind to me and I love her too. I do not think we can ever really lose her."

Later, Carina sat and looked out of her window. Her thoughts drifted. Of course her trip must be postponed; that was not even a question. Her mother was sick. Her father worked too hard, building, fishing, and caring for her mother. When did all of this change? She thought of her party and dancing. Then a greater picture came in. It was of the One Great Giver, and his spring of life rushed around her feet. Then he handed her a pearl, its light unfading, of great value. However, she was unable to take it in her hand. She held a pearl already, one dark and heavy. Then she remembered Malwell's gift. It had been hidden away in a small box, and she had buried it in her mother's garden. It had been there all this time, just under the earth where Eldoris liked to sit and plant and tend. Carina felt suddenly sick with the remembering. She went outside to dig up the box, but as she did, she recoiled at the thought of touching it, of seeing it. What if she found it beautiful instead of terrible and could not be done with it? She rushed to her father.

He was sitting in his chair by the fire leafing through an old book. She came and knelt down by him and looked up into his face.

"My Star, this must be serious. What is it now?"

"I must tell you something. Only it is difficult, but so important. On the night of the party, you were there when he, he asked me to dance. When we stopped, he gave me something. I did not mean to hide it from you. There was just so much happening, and later you said to be wary of him and his stories, but he did come to my aid. So I hid it. It was just a simple necklace. I thought it could do no harm. I was wrong, so wrong. It has been here with us all along. I am sorry. Forgive me, Father, please."

With that she began to cry and her father took her to his heart.

"My child, if I had warned you more, spoken to you of such things, sooner. We have all been troubled, and your mother so sick. I am supposed to protect you it is true, but not by hiding things and now see how it has become. I should ask you to forgive me also. Will you?"

"There is nothing to forgive, Father."

"Then let's be done with it. Where is this thing?"

"In the garden, in mother's garden, just at the foot of the lattice."

So Calder found the box.

"What will you do with it, Father?"

"It must be destroyed, my child."

Calder walked down close to the river. He built a small fire and threw the thing in it. It began to glow. Then it shattered like glass and melted into the fire, sending up dark fumes, which were blown away by the river breezes. Then Calder went down to the river and brought up bucket after bucket of water until the last of it was washed away and all was clean again. "I don't believe it was even a real pearl after all," he said. "No," Carina added. "I should think not."

They went in to tell Eldoris and found her sleeping with the first look of real rest upon her face that they had seen in many days. From that moment, she began to recover.

 Ara

During the weeks when Carina was preparing to leave, Malwell was also preparing. Another ship arrived with more men and cargo. It became increasingly secretive so no one knew exactly how many men there were, or how many of the town's people supported him, or even where all his soldiers came from. Malwell was indeed seen less and less out on the streets, but his presence was felt more and more. Postings of stories translated from "Malwell's Book" were plastered around town and scattered on the breeze. Carina and Ara sometimes collected them, for the fire under the fish.

They enjoyed their time together and tried not to think of the parting to come. "Besides," Ara added, "Father and I will be leaving soon too. We've been stocking up for a journey of our own. We haven't given up on my brother. We mustn't, and with what we now know of Malwell, we thought to follow his trail backward until it meets with our own. But I would so love to be able to go with you."

"I wish you could come with me too."

"Things seem all scattered, Carina. Who will bring it all together?"

"I don't know, Ara. I don't even know who I am."

Ara hugged her. "You are Carina, my dearest friend. And what else would you rather be?"

Carina smiled, but her heart ached. "I don't deserve such a friend."

"Well…that may be true. But you are stuck with me all the same, I am afraid." Ara smiled and Carina smiled too. But that did not keep back the little tear that spilled over.

"Now, dear, shall we take your new boat out on the river and give it another try?" Ara was really not so fond of boating, but hoped to cheer Carina. So the two readied the boat and made a short run upriver, and then down, before crossing to the other bank. There they met a group of people picnicking, although it hardly seemed a party. Carina heard one man whisper, "Quiet now, someone's about."

Then a lady replied, "Oh, don't be such a fool. I know that one, walking there, that one is Calder and Eldoris' daughter and certain to be no secret spy of Malwell."

"Ah, but what of the other? It'd be just like a spy to be where a spy's most likely not to be you see. These days who is to know who is on what side anyway? Best to be careful, my dear."

Carina and Ara smiled, and wished the group a good day.

"See there!" added the man. "That proves it!"

"Oh it proves nothing, but that they have manners better than you have!"

But it did prove something to Carina and Ara.

"Carina, do you think there are spies?"

"Honestly, Ara, I do not know. I would not put it past him at all. But then, to be afraid of one's own friends and neighbors, even one's own shadow, is a terrible thing and if that is how people feel then he has done quite a lot of his job already, spies or no."

"I suppose," Ara added, "if people knew their friends and neighbors, it seems to me, they would treat them a good deal better, even as you and your family have done for mine. But I know now not all neighbors are so good. Carina, I haven't studied with Altea nearly so long, but my mother used to tell me some of the same stories. I think she believed them and now, with my brother lost, it is just me and Papa, and I think, well, we need something to hang on to. I mean, whatever happens, I'm with you all the way, no matter how far apart we may be or what happens. Whatever comes, however things appear, spies or no, you can trust me, and I shall always trust you." Somehow Ara's simple assurance gave Carina so much joy and strength.

The First Leaving

B ack in the village, to counter his meetings and his fear, Altea gathered those who still believed in the old stories. They meet outside of town beyond Calder's house, in the woods, near a stream. The times together were simple. There were songs and stories and sometimes fruit from someone's orchard or a loaf of freshly baked bread. There were a few families who had been "encouraged" by Malwell to sell their homes. They were needed for great things, he had told them and the good of all. Although they were given a few gold coins and such, it still left them homeless. They were taken in by others. There were two whole families living at Altea's.

Malwell's giving of the tainted black pearl was a strong reminder of what they dealt with now. Still, they rejoiced that Eldoris was growing strong. So it was that as the day for Carina's departure came, there was sadness at her leaving, but also a defiant sort of hope.

Eldoris had made for Carina an outfit which was reminiscent of the one she had come in as a child. It was a long shirt with an overlapping neckline, which crossed from Carina's right shoulder under her left arm. Another ribbon stretched across her shoulder at a countering angle. She also wore a belt, an arm band, and a head band. These were Carina's own updates. The pants were long, but made to be hooked up if need came to walk in water; this it usually did with Carina. The whole of the suit was a bright turquoise with edges of dark trim. It was lovely, but simple. Eldoris thought Carina looked so like she did when she arrived, especially as she stepped into her boat. She also wished someone could go with her. Yet, was it not Carina's journey?

Other provisions were loaded. She carried the pages and lastly her bow and quiver full of new arrows and her spear were handed in.

As Calder said to Eldoris, "for hunting and fishing and such."

He had also warned her, away from her mother, that she may face real danger and not the least of those, Malwell's men. Yet, Carina's leaving went well, other than the tears, with only Eldoris and Calder present. None of Carina's other friends or even Altea were there so as not to bring more attention than necessary. The official terms of Carina's passage had been a "neighborly visit upriver."

The day before she was to set out Carina went to take leave of a few of her neighbors and of course Ara and her father and then Altea.

Tobin and Ara had prepared a sort of farewell tea for her. She entered and was surprised by the table set with their best dishes and even two small parcels were on the table. Tobin welcomed Carina and looked at Ara too. "We do not like this parting, but we want this to be a happy day and with that in mind we celebrate friendship." They sat down to the celebration. Of course there were stories to be told. Tobin regaled them with tales of his childhood and the girls laughed.

"Time for gifts?" Tobin asked this as he finished laughing at one of his own stories.

"You did not have to do this."

"But you like gifts and this is a special occasion," answered Ara.

"Mine first," said Tobin. Carina lifted the paper wrapping and found a little carving of two girls walking arm in arm.

"It is beautiful. It is just perfect. Thank you, Tobin."

"I saw you and Ara walking home one day." Then he smiled, "Now Ara's."

Carina opened a box to reveal a strand of ribbon. It was embroidered with vines and flowers.

"It is so beautiful! Did you make this?"

"Yes. I thought it would look lovely in your hair and then you can think of me."

"Ara and Tobin, I shall always think of you. Thank you so much for all of this, for your friendship, for everything."

Then Tobin began to clear the dishes so that Ara and Carina could wander out into the small garden plot. They spoke of many things. It would be difficult to recount them all.

At last Tobin came out to join them. There were tears and smiles. After Carina left, Tobin wrapped his arms around Ara. "She'll not be away too long, I wager, my darling girl."

"It isn't that. Not only that, Papa. I know she will return. I just feel there is more in the journey. I feel there is so much more." She paused and added softly, "I have a certain tingling in my shoulders. It has happened only a few times before."

Tobin nodded and held her more closely. "We shall see what comes. I have not your senses on things to come, but I do know a true friendship when I see one. Let us trust in that." They watched Carina tread her way toward Altea's.

"Ah, my child!" Altea greeted her with a knowing smile. "You come to say farewell?"

"Yes, Eldress, but I think I shall miss you too much to leave."

"Yes, child, but it is not only me you fear to leave is it?"

"No, it is mother and father and Ara and Tobin and many others in the town. Even though mother is getting better she is still weakened from the...you know, and there is Ara and her father too. Also, I am afraid of what my father may do, if it comes to it. I have so longed to understand my coming. But now I think I do not understand my going. The town has changed so much since the coming of, since last spring, I mean. I feel as though when I return, it will never be the same. Do you see this, Altea? Do you know what is to be done? Should I stay?"

"Oh Carina, always so many questions with you. How I shall miss it. Do you think all things will stay still just because you do? I am not sure what is to become of us. I never really did know that. I do know that things have changed and will change, but whether for good or bad seems to depend greatly on us. As for you, you do have a journey to make; although, you may find it not to be the one that you had planned. Carina, this town has stopped its ears and closed its eyes to the truth, in favor of Malwell's twistings. They began in hospitality and curiosity, but they have strayed so far, and it will take an act of great love and perhaps great pain to stir them to themselves and make them see and hear again. Those who follow through in this may pay a great price, but they will also offer a great gift."

"Altea, you speak in riddles, when I ask for answers. How am I to follow?"

"Not how, child, only which way, that is the decision that lies before you. Now come, it is nearly time for you to go, and I want to see one more sunset with you here."

They went to the back balcony that looked toward the mountains and the great forests of the north. Yellow roses hung with spinning green vines around the dark railings. Altea swept around the great dark cape that always followed her. "Carina, there is one more thing I can give you before you set out" and out from under the cape spread a solitary wing, a beautiful dark wing with bright purple, shining in the dying light. "Yes, even I am one of the winged ones. We fly in these lands still, although with greater care. You may see many things you did not believe, and you may have to believe many things, which you do not see."

Carina thought much on Altea's words and wondered why she had not thought of it before. She did not understand what this thing was that should make the people see and hear again. Altea had told her that she was to go on a journey. Perhaps it was best for her to go. Perhaps, somehow, her leaving was a part of this change. Carina so wanted to under-stand her past, her dreams, her other language, the strange pages that looked ripped from a book. She wanted to know who she was.

The Stand

In Malwell's room he sat going over some papers. He flung some into the fire. He was interrupted by one of his men who brought a report. He listened and then sent him away. "Guards, bring in Lieutenant Nuewell." When he stood before the Captain, Malwell continued, "I have just had a report of an unauthorized vessel heading upstream. Why was it not stopped?"

"I checked all of the papers, Captain. All vessels were cleared."

"Bring the documents, then." Malwell did not look happy as he saw the name and the council's seal. Then his grin returned. "Yes, I see here papers for a neighborly visit upriver, for one Carina, daughter of Calder and Eldoris. Now, does this seem like something we can allow? The poor child may come to harm, alone on the river, and that would be a terrible thing, which we should *try* to stop."

"Yes, Captain."

"Let's see. Safe passage upriver and if she decides to return home, that's hardy upriver now is it, and we would not want her to get herself into trouble, now would we?"

"No, sir. Should I try to warn her, Sir?"

"Oh Nuewell, don't try to think. Simply listen and do. Now, see what else you can find out about where she is going and why. In the meantime, perhaps someone should pay her parents a visit. I must have answers. See to it. Now leave me."

Carina was not more than a day gone when some of Malwell's men came to Calder's house asking questions and rummaging about. Altea was visiting Eldoris, and they both greatly protested. But the guards barged in without concern. "What's this contraption?" one asked as he stumbled into the cellar and into Carina's own boat. "It's nothing but an old boat. We do fish you know? And what rights have you to be here? Tell me."

Calder was out in the forest just then. When the men found that Calder was not at home and Eldoris was not willing to answer many questions, at least not to their liking, they took her and Altea into custody and on their way to Malwell's headquarters they passed through the town square. A commotion grew as people realized what was happening. They called to others and soon Calder was there as well. Calder demanded to know what the charges were. But they would not answer. They only said that Malwell had asked that they be brought to see him.

Both Altea's and Eldoris' hands had been tied. Altea was used to walking with the aid of her walking stick and, in the pushing of the crowd by Malwell's guards, it was knocked from her hands, and she fell. Eldoris tried to steady her, but one of the guards struck Eldoris, sending her to the ground. Calder rushed in to pick her up along with Altea and was himself hit by the guard. He struck back. A fight began, and soon both guards were on the ground and Eldoris and Altea untied. Calder then stood up on a bench in the square and in the midst of the crowd he began to speak.

"You see what they have done, what they have been doing, and what we have let them do. Now they tie us up without reason and bind and strike our wives and widows. Malwell is evil. He twists the truth for his own ends, and cruelly beats down those who would stand for truth. We must not allow this. We must stand together against him. Tell him the truth. Do not listen to his twisted tales. Do not entertain them in the least. Do not let him twist and mangle what is good; do not let the truth of the old stories fade. Tell them—"

Then, in the midst of this speech, as people listened and grew quiet, a single arrow flew in a great arch into Calder's arm. He turned to see where it had come from and another arrow flew into his leg. Eldoris ran and tried to reach Calder as a third arrow sailed into her leg. She too fell at the moment that the forth and final arrow sank Calder to the ground. A great cry went up from Eldoris, from Altea, and from many in the crowd that had gathered in the town square.

As Carina rowed up stream, she felt a wave pass through the waters like the falling of a great weight and she felt a stab in her heart, like the plunge into too cold water.

Eldoris held Calder just for a moment. Then one of Malwell's men pushed her away, even as she grasped at Calder and pushed back at the guard. Another guard joined the struggle.

"You sure he's not dead?" one asked.

"Well, not quite yet, remember, like he said?"

The other responded, "Now is it to the river?" This is all Eldoris heard as a few of the men held her back. Then more guards came and the great commotion grew mob-like and impossible. Everything seemed to become muted and strange as she watched them pull Calder away and she could do nothing. But she watched him until he disappeared into the crowd. She thought, once, his eyes met hers. Then he was gone and the guards threw her to the ground.

The crowd rushed to Malwell's new residence, still under construction. Its gates were closed, and well-armed guards gave protest from within the safety of the high walls. The door warder for Malwell said that the great leader was not there, and he would attend to this rabble on his return. Of course he was sorry for such confusion as happened when he was not there to lead his people and many other such things that the crowd grew weary at listening to him and turned back to the square, still in protest. The council was not sitting that day, and the door warder there only directed their complaints back to Mawell's wise authority.

Eldoris, Altea, Tobin, Ara, and others searched for Calder, but to no avail. At last, on the edge of water, Eldoris found his belt. It was one she had woven for him. She sank to her knees. A trickle of blood soaked through the hastily made bandage on her leg and ran into the stream. She cried into the waters. They lapped up around her, singing a low, beautiful song.

Upstream

Carina pulled the boat up along the shore, on a quiet sandy bank, and made camp for the night. She tried to rest, but found little comfort for her aching heart. She knew not why and thought it was, perhaps, only the thought of leaving. She continued the next day. The current was strong and she made little progress. That night she camped again and the next day she made it to the town upriver. When she went into the village, there was a great crowd interested in some news. Carina inquired of a merchant what all of this was about.

The shopkeeper thinking her, by her dress, a stranger from farther upriver answered her, "Oh, I wouldn't bother too much about it miss. It was only something about a bit of brawling from a town downriver. A rider just came in from Keldalee telling of a fight. He said that several had been injured and at least one missing, most likely killed, but I expect that one'll turn up too. It's probably nothing to be concerned over. Only he said we might expect company as the new ruler there, a Captain Malfell, Balwell, something or other like that, was sending for more supplies from upriver."

Carina's heart sank. She knew that pain, the wave.

"Miss, miss, are you all right? Can I help you?"

She shook her head, "No, sir, I am afraid not—wait."

"Yes, miss?"

"Perhaps you can. You see I know some good people in the town you speak of, and I know that this new ruler, one Malwell, is not to be trusted. If his ships do come here and there is any way to stop them, or even hinder or confuse them, it would be of great help to me and those I care for."

The man, a father himself, seeing the bright tears in her eyes promised to do anything he could and set about finding trusted friends who could help him in this plan to stall the ships. She hoped it would be nothing, but she felt in her heart differently. Perhaps it had all been a mistake. She had barely begun this journey, and already things seemed so wrong.

In the searching of her home, Malwell's men had found a map of the river marked with the stops on Carina's planned trip. Riders were sent to each of these towns to await her coming. But she would miss their greetings. She turned her ship toward home.

The Quick Return

She came in the dark of night. She could see just barely, with the light of the moon, as she passed, what looked like the beginnings of some construction on the banks of the river. She landed her boat and hid it as best she could. Then she gathered her things and crept to her mother and father's window. There was but one candle; Carina tapped lightly and waited. Her mother cautiously came and quickly pulled her in through the window. She clattered in with bow and spear. Eldoris held her tightly.

"What are you doing here? How I hoped you would be far, far away."

"I heard news upriver."

"What news?"

"Something of a fight and several injured and one missing. But even before that, I felt a great wave, a great wave of pain swept over my heart. I had to come back. Where is Father so late?"

Eldoris wiped her face as tears fell down onto Carina.

"Then it was him," Carina said.

They sat there in the dark for a moment, just breathing together.

At last Carina made them some tea and toast, seeing her mother's leg. Then she lit the fire, and slowly Eldoris was able to recount to her all that had happened and what followed.

"Carina, if you could have but seen him. No, I would not have wanted you to see it all. If you could have just seen his face; it was brilliant and his words said with such love. The people listened like I have not seen in so long. There were tears in his eyes and when they saw it, they saw the truth at last. Many have come back. It was his stand that brought the awakening of many."

After this they talked of other times for a while. Then Carina asked about the construction on the riverbank. Eldoris did not know what it was, but had heard rumors that Malwell had instructed his men to build some type of bridge or barrier to control traffic on the river, entering and leaving the bay. Then Carina added that she had heard that more ships were being sent for to aid Malwell and added what she had told the merchant upriver. Eldoris told her that they must get this message to Altea, and so Carina must go to the Eldress' house, by the long road, through the woods.

"Yes, of course. But mother, why is Altea not here with you? Why are you here alone?"

"My child, I am wounded beyond what I can say. Calder was, is, my heart's love. But I have not been alone. I shall never be alone and neither will you, my love. Now go."

As she approached Altea's, she could see a figure waiting outside. She moved with great caution to get a better look. He was dressed in a dark cloak, deep brown, as of worn leather, and his hood hid much of his face. Yet, Carina could see his bright eyes.

Then he turned to Carina and held her gaze with his own. Carina heard his voice speaking to her, "Know that what your father did has given life to many. Perhaps also you will find later on that things are not as you think they are, but as they really are and that this is a far better thing." Then he beckoned to her, "Child, come inside." She hesitated and then stepped out into the light. It was Elias. He reached out and took her hand.

She told them of her news. He smiled softly when she told them how she had set out upriver, only to turn around.

"Carina," Altea spoke with unusual concern, "You see you must leave again. You must get away. You know too much of the truth and," but Elias turned toward her and she left off. Then she finished, "We do not know what Malwell may do."

"Why must I go, and where?"

"Carina," Altea pleaded. "You simply must get away and now, and do you have," she lowered her voice even more, "the book?"

"Yes, but I do not understand. Why would I be in danger more than any one else? Why cannot I stay and help?"

Then Elias smiled and spoke, "Carina, it is true you will be in some danger if you stay here now, and yet, that is not why you must go. The book is your legacy and you must see it safe until the appointed time. For now, that means getting it out of this village." Then he took her two hands in his, "Go in strength, daughter, in freedom, and in peace." Then he bowed to Altea and was gone.

"Oh Altea, what is to be done?"

"Oh child, always questions. Did you not hear Elias? He has always been with us. Though we do not always see him, it is true. You remember, The Spring that comes of The Source?"

"Altea, that man was Elias, an old friend. He has traveled through our village many times before. He knows much of the old stories, but so do you and so do I."

"Yes, we know much. We do not know all. There are many things yet to learn."

"But I thought the spring was a fountain?"

"Oh child, The Source gives so much more than just a fountain, but all fountains and no fountains, water and words, and love. The One Great Giver gives all life and all stories. He is always with us, although it may not always be how we expect. He is truth."

"Altea. I do not understand this and so much has happened."

"Oh child," she breathed as she slid one beautiful wing out from beneath her cloak and wrapped it about Carina. "Yes, it has been a heavy day for you, and it will weigh heavily still. You must remember the words of Elias, your friend, and think on my love for you and your mother's, and Ara's and even your father's. Those are true and real and will help you. You should be on your way, my child." She paused and smiled at Carina. "I am not used to being in a hurry. But there are still many things that are not as they appear, and you will want to talk to your mother more. Dawn will come swiftly, and you should be on your way before then. Be careful now and remember the ship that brought you here. My child, remember you are loved and shall be helped. There will come a time when light shall shine out clearly. It is not yet come. It will. And child, be careful on the river. Yet, there are many branches before the sea."

Carina said good-bye to Altea once again. She hardly knew what happened, even as it happened.

Leaving Again

From Altea's, Carina had suddenly had the idea to go a little ways upstream, get back to her boat first, and then go home by way of the river. But when Carina drew near to the place she had landed her own boat, she realized that some of Malwell's guards stood between her and it. She turned to go home and saw more of them blocking her path. She was caught, but yet unseen, only dawn would be approaching soon. Then she saw one of Malwell's smaller crafts used for crossing the river and making small runs up and down. It was close at hand. If she could make her way to it and then back to her house, perhaps she could wait it out. She waded quietly to the boat and seized a dark cloak which was hanging over the side. She lifted the rope and pushed the craft out into the river. She tried to remain calm, to think it was all a dream, and not to think of what might happen if she were caught.

She rounded the new construction and was at the far side of the river. The current picked up, and there was a gust of wind. Then she heard a scraping sort of sound. She had crossed back too soon and come close to Malwell's dock in the dark and had certainly run upon some of the unfinished work. One of the men on lookout shone a lantern out over the edge. He called down to her, "Who's there and what's your business?"

She didn't answer, but struggled with the boat. It was not moving.

"There's no one who has permission to be here at this time. Do you hear?"

She heard from above the one man yell to another and then the sounds of someone coming closer. In the faint light, Carina began to distinguish a few forms and then lanterns and then more. She was left with no option. She threw off the borrowed cloak and dove headfirst into the water.

The moon shone out. The current took her down, swirling and turning everything blue, then green, then gray, then dark. Then, just as suddenly, she seemed to feel a push. Then it was gray, then green, then blue. Then the firm grit of the sand met her. The water brought her up on her own shore. There was a boat already there and someone waiting with it. How had they managed so quickly? But then, with relief, she realized it was her mother, standing with the boat Carina had arrived in.

"Quickly now, it is ready to depart, loaded with what I could find and what you will need. Here is your quiver and arrows and the spear still; but no matter. The current has brought you safely and given you a few moments of time."

"But Mother, how did you know?"

"Carina, I had a visitor while you were gone. I too have seen Elias. But you, you must go now. Even for a simple act of desperation you will certainly be accused as a thief, and you have no papers for passage downriver. Malwell's courts are just that, they are his now. You are, you are a pirate I'm afraid, my love, and Malwell will not look favorably on it, the way I do. But, perhaps, he need not know all now. Go quickly my child, my love, our star."

And so Carina stepped into the boat and it carried her away.

Even as the dawn came and swept over, Carina felt her night deepening. She felt the weight of her aloneness for the first time, and the realization came that even if she should find the answer to her questions, if the writing in her book were to be made clear and Malwell defeated by its truth, her father was gone and if all these things did not come together, she was a runaway now, and how could she even think of returning? What would she return to? She wept and fell into fitful sleep only to wake and remember and cry again. The light of her stars was veiled and yet the sun would not shine out either. It was weary and long with only the sounds of the water. If only she understood them. What if, after all, it was just a story? She spent the early morning in doubts passing through a fog, little knowing where she was. All that kept her awake was the certainty that if she slept now there was even less chance of sleep during the night. But thoughts of her father assailed her. At last she gave in and let them flow through her memory.

Even as Carina sank into despair, the waters buoyed her on and still they sang. Finally, she slipped out of the boat and into the waters. She floated along beside her boat. She felt the pain of loss and she allowed herself to also hear the waters and, though the pain was lessened none, she knew somehow that she was not alone. She knew that the waters mourned with her and shared her pain. It was the strangest sort of comfort simply to know she was not alone in her aching. It seemed as though the waters gave themselves to wrap all around her, carrying her burden as their own, carrying her as their own.

The Chase

The growing light showed Carina a country that she was less familiar with. The marsh forests had begun. This was why travel came and went by way of the waters and why there was not a town closer to the bay. The forests were dense and supposedly full of bogs and sink holes. They had always been considered unsafe by the people of the village, although there were paths to follow, if one were willing, and knew the way, Altea had told her. She began to wonder just a little what would become of her. But she had not long to think.

As the fog lifted, not only could Carina see but she could be seen, and she noticed for the first time another craft behind her. She began to row, but the other vessel had spotted her already. Then she heard the whizzing sounds of arrows passing her boat and the thud as a few struck the thick arch of the ship. She was safe in the boat as long as they were behind her. But what happened if they should overtake her? No, she must get away.

Then she heard a splash and noticed someone climbing up the far left bank of the river. Carina tried to steer the boat away and arrows continued to fly from behind her. Then an arrow came across the boat. Carina stood poised and took her own bow and sent an arrow into the arm of the man on the bank in front of her. He fell. Then, from behind, an arrow pierced her arm just below the shoulder. She fell into the boat as another arrow flew right through the space where she had been standing.

She could see that there were more trees and vines up ahead. She remembered that Altea had told her that the river sometimes branched off. She rowed and noticed the current swirling around her. Suddenly, she came into another patch of fog. Then her boat made a sharp turn toward the right, and the branches gave way around her and then closed behind her. She strained her eyes, but could see little. In the quiet mistiness she strained her ears to hear. The sounds grew fainter, and at last she was sure that the other boat was in fact no longer following her. She had broken off somehow into one of the wanderings of the Blythe. She did her best to remove the arrow from her arm and wrapped it with a bit of cloth. It ached horribly, but she could do little else for it.

As the mist pulled away, a diffused yellow and green sort of light opened up. She looked around and saw that she was now floating slowly, but steadily, down a very different stream. From its banks, and even in the water, grew up great trees curving and bending to make a roof and long branches and small fluttering green leaves hung down. The gnarled roots grew up through the water, making loops and lanes in the marsh-like surroundings. Yet, it was not a dark place. Around these larger trees grew vines, and along the edge grew other ferns and flowers of all hues. The light filtered down through the trees to the very ground level of dappled leaves. It pulsed with life and the songs of birds and the murmuring of the waters. Even the very air seemed awake with life. Carina thought she had never seen such a place before. She rested in its peace and warmth.

The Break in the Stream

Perhaps now we should see what had become of the other vessel on the river. Malwell's men did not actually know that Carina had been home. They did know that someone had tried to commandeer one of Malwell's smaller vessels and had run upon the unseen construction in the river. They also knew that someone had escaped their grasp and would bring down the reprisal of Malwell's malevolence on their heads. So when they spotted the sign of a vessel leaving without official permission, they followed. This was all they had to go on, apart from his dark cloak found in the waters and his bold act. He must certainly be a daring criminal.

They had gone downstream a good while without seeing anything until at last the fog had lifted. After a few volleys of arrows, Malwell's men felt sure of their success until they rolled into another patch of fog and lost sight of the ship. When they came out, the ship was not there either. Then a strange current pulled them off to the left. There was a bend in the river, and as much as they fought, it did no good against the strength of the water. They were sent off down the river; but not to the sea. Instead their course lay on a long and winding river with a lake at the end. However, it would be quite a while before they would arrive and discover their predicament. This would give them time to think of their story of the fierce pirate, in his swift vessel, who was yet wounded, and then dismissed as unworthy of further chase.

Carina, in the meantime, at last dozed a little and when she woke, she found that the stream was widening. She could also see through the trees at last. She also noticed a dull, but strong, ache coming from her wounded arm. She unwrapped it and bathed it with cool water from the stream. She did this several times. This did quite a bit to soothe it; yet, the wound was deep. Carina pulled some bread and dried apple slices from her store of food. She realized that she had not eaten all day and had not eaten much at all since she had left her own home, which reminded her, of course, of home, Ara, Altea, her mother, and finally her father. She looked into the water. It looked cleaner and bluer and somehow ever softer. A few tears fell from her face in the water, sinking down. In the clarity of the water, she wondered if it were possible that her father could still be alive, somehow.

She stared into the water and tried to listen. She reached out her arm to touch the surface, and she thought she saw something move. She looked again and was almost sure. "Of course it's just a fish," she thought, but then she was not sure. It looked like, well, like a person, there was a face, with bright eyes, smiling and moving and swimming. She leaned closer, trying to see, trying to hear. Then she did hear, a splash, but it was her own as she toppled over the edge of the boat. Carina was a very strong swimmer, but when she came to herself, she realized her arm was still quite sore, and she was rather incapable of using it as she would have liked. She reached for the edge of boat and did her best to hold on. She saw a landing and the current pulled her along. Finally, she and the boat found themselves resting on a grassy bank. Carina was exhausted and allowed herself, just for a moment, to close her eyes.

Aldwyn's House

When Carina woke, she found herself not on a riverbank, but in a cozy bed, surrounded by soft feather quilts. At her window grew wild roses. The fragrance drifted in on the breeze. There was another lovely smell too, which seemed to be coming from the pink flower petals in a saucer by her bed. The lamp on the table told her it was dark without. She looked up from the bed and, as her eyes adjusted to the low light, she could see that she was in a small room. There were shelves of books and three paintings on the wall across from her. One was of a glowing sea, the second of sky above an old forest, and the third of a green and golden field. Through the doorway she could see a hall and just a bit of light coming from another room. There was also music drifting in from somewhere. A lady entered the room. She was dressed in flowing hues of pale pinks, layered, and tied around her neck were the strings of her cloak, and the darker hues of green fell behind her and trailed at her feet. Carina thought she looked like a forest flower. Then the lady smiled at Carina and walked noiselessly toward the bed.

"You are wondering where you are I should think. Do not fear. You are safe here, and all is well, or shall be made well further in. You have come to the house of Aldwyn, and I am his niece, Ancelin. My Uncle Aldwyn found you by the bank and has since brought your boat here. You are welcome to stay and rest as long as you need. It seems you've had some sort of adventure already and more may be in store, so questions will make a stay for a while. When you are ready, I will bring you something to eat. Now rest." And saying so, she lightly stirred the petals with her fingers, touched Carina's forehead, and was gone.

When Carina woke again she was given a bowl of some wonderful steamy broth and some freshly baked bread, warm and soft on the inside with golden crust. The music played again as Carina ate and Ancelin sat by her side, smiling peacefully and sketching pictures in a little book. Every now and then she turned the book in such a way that Carina could better see it. There were trees and fields and a stream, then water, swirling waters, the sea, then islands, ruins, and stars in the sky, then storms, but the sun at last. All the time, Ancelin never said a word. She only looked intently at Carina and at her work in turn. When Carina had finished eating, she felt much better than she had in quite a while. Ancelin smiled again and finally spoke, "As you are feeling better, my uncle will be in to see you soon." As she left she took the tray, but left the book of sketches by Carina's bed.

Soon the music from the other room stopped and a man came in, his reed flute in hand. His face was weathered, but full with smiling. His eyes were bright and his hair was silvery white as was his beard, which grew in waves just past his chin. He seemed old and young at the same time and Carina, having never known a grandfather, imagined this must be what it was like. Aldwyn took up the chair that Ancelin had left vacant.

"Greetings child, and welcome." Carina thought his words were warm like his smile, like the yellow light.

"Thank you, Sir. You and your niece have been most kind to me, only a stranger, and I feel I shall never be able to repay you."

"You are most welcome, and there is no need to repay what is freely given. You are a guest here." He paused, "What is your name, child?"

"Carina, Sir."

"Ah, Carina," he continued, "I see you are on a journey of sorts. I found you and your boat, which is also quite safe, mind you. I have done my best to mend the arrow holes in both it and you. Though the craft is made of a most unusual and strong wood, I fear your arm is not so hardy, through no fault of your own. The arrow that went into you was tipped with the poison of the Malbraken Leaf. It was well for you that you removed it as you did and cleaned it so well. Less of the poison was left to enter you, and now you understand how a little arrow can make such trouble. Ah, but what sort of villain would use such a weapon at the back of a lone traveler?"

He seemed to ask the question more to himself than to Carina, and as he did so, his head dropped and his smile faded, just for a moment.

Then he smiled again and said, "You will be much recovered in few days time, I think. Still, I would feel better if you would stay with us and heal more fully before you try to travel further. You will be safe here for as long as you need."

"Safe," the word sounded so good to Carina's ears, and Aldwyn was so confident in saying it. Did she need to keep going? Perhaps she could just stay here and wait. What would she be waiting for? She doubted even more that she could find anything that would be of help. Finally, she told Aldwyn of her strange journey. She cried as she remembered what her mother had said of her father. She closed her eyes. But if she would have looked, she would have seen, too, in Aldwyn's eyes, bright tears falling as he reached out his hand and took her own.

"Child, you have suffered so much already and it is just the start. You will go on, and there will be sun and kind currents after the storms and rocks. But," he added with a smile, "Is not there some more to your story? You see, I have left out a part of my story too. I am an old friend of your Eldress Altea, and she sent word to me many months ago, that you would be coming to see us, although she could not say quite when."

"But how could she have known when I did not know myself?"

"There are many things that wise ones know when we do not know ourselves. There is still much of Altea you do not know, nor I. I can tell you that she has had her own troubles and adventures and has, at last and not too late, learned to listen well. She has also learned to perceive and to understand and to believe some things that others dare not dream of."

Carina had never thought much of what Altea's life was before she knew her. She had always believed that Altea was wise. She knew from her mother that she had not always lived in the village, and yet it was Altea's words and stories that had captivated Carina's heart and mind. She had hardly stopped to think about Altea's past. She too had been someone else, somewhere else. She had never thought about how she came to be so wise.

The Water's Voice

The next day Carina was well enough to venture out of doors. Ancelin brought to her baskets filled with various plants and showed her which ones were good for eating and which ones were good for healing various pains and illnesses. Then Carina, sitting on the porch, helped Ancelin to sort the plants and flowers and tie them in bundles as Ancelin hung them from a string to dry. They soon made a sort of garland all around them, some tapping on the porch eaves in the breeze. Then Ancelin pulled a flower from one of the baskets and handed it to Carina.

"It's beautiful, and what does it do?"

"Ah, that one is lovely and very important. It goes in your hair."

And they laughed together, as Carina had not laughed in many days. In the afternoon, she again listened to the flute's song and fell asleep with Ancelin's book of sketches in her hands.

It was with great interest and a sort of reverence that Aldwyn pondered over Carina's book in the coming days. They looked over it together and he smiled at her. "I never thought I should live to see such a day. Your Eldress Altea was correct.

This is written in the ancient script of the waters. There are few on land who know it now. Some I can teach to you. But this book, it has been torn from something else." He took from a shelf another volume, old too, but not so old as the torn book. "This tells the story of what we call The Battle of Lockwood Hill and The Sundering of the Great Book. I suppose you have heard the story?"

"Yes, from the Eldress."

"Perhaps, you would like to read it still?"

"Yes, please." So as Carina read, Aldwyn sat in thought with her book. With each page turned, his eyes brightened more into tears. Finally, Carina looked up at him.

"Then you think this book, my book, is one of the three pieces?"

"I do believe it is so, my child. I do not know how, but I do believe it. I imagine Altea even suspected it, but she is also wise enough to keep her own counsel."

"Then, what must I do?"

"As the story goes, it seems, you are now its keeper and it is up to you to decide. You see, you have the first piece, the one that gathers the others."

The next day Aldwyn took Carina sailing in his own boat. He rowed up stream so that they could float back. As he did, he and Carina talked of the old stories. Then he landed in a little cove on the far shore, while Ancelin sat sorting flowers across the stream.

"Carina," said the deep, soft voice, "I want you to get out of the boat now."

"Sir?"

"I'll help you, of course. I just want you to stay on the shore for a bit."

"But where will you be, and what shall I do?"

"I'll be just across the stream and you, you my child, may listen to the waters in peace."

Carina had not known Aldwyn long and yet sitting on the bank she felt she had nothing to do but to heed his words and wait for his return. If he told her to do anything she was sure, somehow, it could only be for her good. She made herself comfortable on the shore leaning up against a fallen tree. Her arm was still weak. Thoughts went diving and swimming through her head. It was nice here, with Aldwyn and Ancelin. She could stay awhile here and it would be safe and well. She thought, "I could go home, but there is Malwell waiting. I may be put in prison or worse, and if mother and Altea tried to hide me, I should only endanger them more. I suppose I could keep going, looking for some sort of help. I have been wounded already and I don't even know if I would find what I'm looking for. It would just be the searching and I don't know the end."

Then she thought of her father and mother, of her home and friends. She thought of her mother's words. Then came a voice as if from the waters translating in her mind, "You must go forward if you want to go back."

"It's foolish." She answered aloud, not even realizing.

"Then be foolish. Be foolish, for the sake of others and for the sake of One greater than yourself. Your wisdom would say protect what little you still have. I tell you lose it all, lose it all to gain something better."

"How and why?"

"Only follow my voice. Now you know it?"

"But I don't. I don't understand. I don't see!"

"Yet, you don't see yet. You will, in time. Now go in strength, daughter, and in peace." There was something so familiar about that voice. Yet, perhaps, it was but a trick of her imagination, only it was certainly not what she would have imagined.

Later Aldwyn returned. He smiled, helped her into the boat, and asked no questions. Carina thought he must have spent much time listening to the waters.

They continued to study the book and Aldwyn begin to teach Carina what he could of its language. She was quick to learn and thought long on his words as well.

For the next few weeks, things went along like this. Ancelin taught her of the flowers and forests and Aldwyn taught her of the waters and their words and ways. On one especially lovely evening they ate outside under the stars and later Aldwyn played his flute as Ancelin and Carina danced, all to the sound of the waters.

That night, as Carina slipped into sleep, she heard the waters in her dreams. She was in a lovely, golden forest between sunset and moonrise. There was a stream and she was following it. As she walked along, she saw a form in a dark cloak. As he pushed back his hood, a light seemed to shine out. He smiled and their paths ran together in the woods. "Do you remember now, child? When you were young? You came along the river in a boat built for one, yet you were not afraid or alone? You were quite small then and still spoke another language, and I spoke it too. Can you still hear it?" He was quiet for a moment and Carina listened. "You must learn to hear it again and to follow it. Follow the stream. Follow the waters to find what you seek." Then he almost seemed to grow into the light reflected by the moon in the mist. He was bright for only a moment and then faded into the light in the darkness. She woke and the dream was gone. The voice, however, lingered.

Parting

The next morning they all had a good breakfast and sat lingering at the table, telling stories and laughing together. After a moment of quiet Carina began, "I suppose you know, then, that I must continue?"

"Yes, we know," answered Aldwyn, "but we were waiting for you to know. It has seemed to pass so quickly your little time with us, and I enjoy the house being so filled. I've enjoyed you being here."

"Then I haven't been a bother, even in my illness?"

"Oh no child, you have been a joy."

"Are you sure you would not like to stay, a while longer?" Ancelin ventured.

"Of course I would. I thought I could just stay here, happily, and that thought has been a great comfort. But I see now, I must go on."

"And the book?" Aldwyn asked.

"I suppose I must do what I can to find out about it. I will do my best to protect it. I know it is valuable and precious."

"Priceless, my child and so are you. You may not think so yet, but you have been given a great gift. Although how it will

106

all unfold is still to be seen, I do believe good is coming. Good is always coming. A wise man once told me this. I try to have the courage to believe it."

With a few more words Aldwyn and Carina embraced as a grandfather might his own granddaughter, for this is how it seemed.

When she was ready, Ancelin walked Carina down to her boat and what wonderful things were inside. Carina had new arrows, a few baskets of food, Ancelin's finely made bread-cakes, dried fruit, and a cloak, not unlike Ancelin's, but thicker for the water's weather and a curious basket that strapped to one's back. Ancelin explained, "Inside are herbs and flowers, and you will know which you may need. There are some for your arm as well, and some you can brew in water and drink. These," she indicated a blue purse tied with green string, "will purify the water that you may always have something to drink. May they serve you well. I would advise, if you do make landfall somewhere, take the basket with you, always, wherever you go."

"Thank you. It is more than I could have thought of for myself."

"There is one more thing. I shall guide you a little ways down the stream and set you off on the right path, if you like. This way to the sea is longer, but certain to be safe."

Safe, again, Carina mused. How could they be so certain in such times? But she only said, "Oh yes, please." And then thought to ask, "But how will you return?"

"That will be easily solved," and she tossed her cloak back and out stretched two long, lovely wings, light pink rimmed with a darker rose color and glints of deep brown and bright green, all glistening in the sun. They had the beauty and lightness of butterfly wings, but with a far greater strength and ability to stretch. Indeed she could have wrapped them around herself if she had wanted or tucked them away as she had been doing.

Carina gasped, "How lovely, like Altea, only pink like the wild roses of the forest."

Ancelin smiled. Then she just lifted up into the air. She lightly kicked her legs, and her soft slippers tied about her ankles showed under her embroidered pants and long light jacket and long sash. She hovered there until Carina was ready too. She obviously enjoyed the breezes flowing around her. Down the river they went. Carina was mesmerized by Ancelin's flight and seeing her wings flutter. She had heard tales all her life of the winged ones, but she had never seen anyone in flight before. She thought of Ara.

Ancelin, perceiving her gaze said, "Ah, they are not just for flying, you know. They are for shelter and protection." Ancelin turned and flew on her back, and the outer portion of her wings was covered with a fine sort of hair. Then she turned again and, into the woods, shot a few fine darts from her wings. "You see," she explained, "they can be dangerous as well. So it is best not to surprise one with wings."

They talked of this and of other things. When at last they came to where the stream branched, Ancelin showed her the way and then added, "May it comfort you to know, that if all goes well, I'll journey to your village in a few days. I have supplies and medicines, and I hope to be able to visit with

Altea. I will tell your mother you are well if am able to get word to her. I have good hope of that. I can take the overland route and need not bother about the dock and bridge on the River Blythe. He has many in his service, but he grows overconfident, thinking himself wise and he makes mistakes. I have been away too long as it is, your coming reminded me. I have much to do still. Farewell, Carina, my friend. May you find not only what you seek, but that which you most need to find."

Ancelin watched as Carina continued down the river, toward the sea, and beyond. From a perch in a branch high in a great tree, she let a few petals fly into the wind and out over the waters. As she did she whispered soft words into the air and then she flew on.

The River

C arina was alone again, but felt it less for the recent company. For two days she traveled down the river, stopping occasionally to rest or pick berries. She knew now which ones. The forest seemed made of dappled light. She even saw a doe drinking with her fawn at the river's edge. She wanted to explore but when she thought to venture too far, the waters called to her. On the third morning she sensed something different in the air. The river, which had been gradually growing wider, opened up into marshlands with scattered, twisting trees and tall grasses waving in the breeze. The waterway made streams and patterns in and out. She followed them with her gaze, over her shoulder. She was so engaged in this activity that she hardly realized that the marshes were fading away, and soon she could see the open bay and beyond a chain of islands. It was beautiful; the spray, the mist, the scent of salt in water, the calls of the gulls. Suddenly she realized how very small she was. The boat washed out into the bay, and the currents grew stronger.

She could see, in the distance, shadowy islands. On one sat Veradis Kel, the old castle. If she had come down the main branch of the river she would have been much closer to it. It seemed, for now, that was not her course.

She endured two days of sailing in the bay. She slept in short intervals, not wholly trusting the current. The beauty of the ocean gave way to a strained sort of endlessness. Carina knew there were more islands, but they became a distant thought. She became a part of the sea, resting when it was calm, tossing when it was restless, and knowing its sounds and sighs and signs.

The wind changed and grew cooler; she knew a storm was coming. She tied down everything as well as she could and wrapped herself well in her cape. She hoped the storm would come and pass quickly. Instead, it trailed on slowly, beginning in dimness and wisps and growing to darkness and water, sheets of water coming down. She could barely see past the edge of the boat and then only with the lightning.

After a bright flash she saw land, an island, and she was headed toward it. She just began to hope. She could see a few lights. They were far, but shining out into the night. She hoped for a village like her own or, perhaps, one which had people like Aldwyn and Ancelin who would take her in. She could almost taste hot broth and feel the firelight. Then a strong breath of wind and a swift current took her away and back into the storm.

She pulled out her oars and fought the current. She knew it must be wrong this time. How could it be right for her to be tossed so in this storm? She struggled against it, weary and wet. But the island was gone, out of reach. Carina collapsed back into the boat. Tears streamed down her face even as the rain ran into the sea.

🌿 The Isle of Stones

At last morning gathered, and the rain stopped. The current pulled her toward another island, although it looked like little more than a grand pile of moss covered rocks leading to a few sad hills to Carina's eyes. Still, it was land. She paddled the boat into a little cove and tethered it around the tip of a rock. "Well, at least you're good for something," she thought of all the stones. She struggled to climb out of the cove. There was not much of a beach, only rocks and more stone. Only they did look a little like silver with the touches of sun, if Carina had noticed. She carried with her the bundle Ancelin had given her. Thinking, if nothing else, perhaps she could find a warm place to dry off and have a sort of picnic. She hardly expected company in such a place. As she walked, she realized there was a valley between the rocks. As she went deeper in, she saw the hills farther back. There was, thankfully, a stream and it ran from a bit of woods. Carina did not want to venture far, but she did want to go where the water was surest to be clean and fresh, if possible. For as much as she loved the sea, she was longing now for land and continued on. It was not like the forests at Aldwyn's, which, though thick with life, still let in light. This forest was dark and breathless. The trees looked tired of holding themselves up. The undergrowth was scanty and covered mostly in moss and fallen needles. Still, there was something about it. There was the feeling that life had once been there and was not altogether gone, only waiting.

Carina soon found herself on what seemed to be a little path running along beside the stream. It crossed a small bridge. She doubted whether she should go on. The path opened up on to what appeared to be a few worn houses. They all looked rather empty and fallen in. She walked past a few of them to see one with a frail trail of smoke coming from the chimney. She turned to go. At that moment she heard the cry of a small child. She stepped closer. She could see through the open window. There was no glass to keep out the wind and the shutters were flying wide open. Inside she could see a woman lying on a small bed. She was wrapped in blankets. Her hair was silvery and her face wrinkled and pale. Beside her sat a woman, younger, with lengths of auburn hair falling over her simple dress of deep brown. She was holding the source of the sound, a baby, in one arm and stroking the head of the lady with the other. Carina, still entranced by the scene, did not notice someone approaching, with careful steps.

"That's far enough. Step away from the window and put your weapons down."

Carina did step slowly and raised her empty hands.

"I have only these arrows for hunting and protection as needed. Clearly my bow is not strung on my finger tips as yours is, and I meant no harm. I am a lone traveler."

"That's a likely…"

But the first speaker was interrupted by another coming up behind him with a bundle of fish in one hand. He seemed older and certainly stood taller. He quickly surveyed the scene and, turning toward the first, asked, "Brother, what is the meaning of this? Put your bow away and do something useful," he added tossing the fish at him, "Can't you see that the *lady* is unarmed and most likely looking for shelter?"

He turned toward Carina, "I'm sorry for his conduct. He seems to think all travelers are like those beyond the rocks. I am sorry. Please, forgive us. My name is Keegan and this rash young fellow is Aidan. Speak to the lady, lad."

"I am very sorry, truly. I'm sure you would forgive one for wanting only to protect his own?"

"Yes, of course I would. My name is Carina, and again I meant no intrusion."

"Of course not," offered Keegan, "but now you are a guest. Please, come in."

Keegan opened the door and the woman stood up with the child still clinging to her, but crying less. I thought I heard voices. She looked at Carina.

"Oh a visitor and you're soaked through! Come sit by the fire."

"Love, this is Carina. Carina this is my wife, Garna."

"I'm pleased to meet you and welcome."

When Carina was comfortable by the fire, Garna offered her a steaming bowl of stew and a bit of bread.

"It's not much. Yet, perhaps it may take the chill off and may you find warmth in this our little home, such as it is."

"Thank you. You are very kind and your home is lovely," replied Carina.

"Well, it's the best kept in the whole village," laughed Keegan. His smile was broad, and he laughed again as he picked up the little girl, and she began to tug at his blond curls. He responded by kissing the top of her head, also covered with curls, but of red blond.

Garna smiled and shook her head.

"Well, at least you're with your family," Carina attempted as she looked around.

"There you are quite right, quite right," Keegan added with another broad smile.

"Speaking of," added Garna, "we've not introduced them all. The lady is Opal and she's not well as you can see. This little one is Ruby and the one there in the corner is Jasper."

Carina realized that she had not even noticed the little boy ducked down in the far corner.

After dinner they gathered around the fire again. It blazed strong in the darkening room. Then they asked Carina if she felt up to telling them of her journey so far. She obliged them with a good tale, although she found some things hard to speak of still and was careful of the book. But they were so taken with the rest of the story, they would hardly have noticed any incongruities.

Then the little ones were put to bed and it was Carina's turn to ask, quite politely, if she might hear their story.

Keegan began, "Well, it's hardly such an adventure, but perhaps it may answer some questions at least. This island here, Carnelian, was once full of precious stones of all kinds.

The first settlers here discovered this, but were careful in the mining and selling. They worked hard and paid fair wages for a day's hard work. They did not value the gems over their lives or the land. Then others moved in and started digging away at the earth. They cut trees mercilessly, caused land-slides, cave-ins, all sorts of trouble. Most moved either to the far side of the island across the mountains or to the island you passed on the way here. They grew rich on the wealth of the island. When it no longer suited them, they left. We are those who remained on this side. Opal could not leave and Garna, my love, would not go without her. Aidan is my brother, not by birth, but by choice. We both lost our parents to the mines and the sicknesses they caused. We escaped with our lives, for their sacrifice. Aidan had no other family here. Garna and I grew up in this village. We were childhood friends. We were married here and Ruby was born here. Jasper came to us, likely escaped from the mines and left behind, though he never said, he doesn't speak or can't. Although he hears and understands everything quite well."

Aidan added, "Yes, I've hardly seen him so interested in anything so much as he was in your story. It was good to see him smile."

"Yes," added Garna, "He seemed so sad when he came and I can't bring myself to think what he may have suffered already and so young."

"And you see," ventured Aidan, "how I'm not quite so terrible. Only there are still some stones left, deep down in dangerous places. Some still come searching, and they are mostly of the kind that would as soon steal as dig, and they sometimes send unlikely looking characters to do the job; although, I am very sorry. I was hasty, as I should have seen you could not have been one of them."

"Perhaps now, our guest would like to rest," Garna added with a smile. "Come Carina, I'll show you to your room. Garna led Carina into the next room and up a winding staircase. I think you'll find everything you need. It isn't much but I've laid out some of my own things for you. They'll be a bit big, but I hope they'll do and," she whispered, "he wouldn't like you to know it, but Aidan has given up this, his loft. He insisted. I think he felt a trifle ashamed about his manner of greeting. Goodnight, sleep well."

After Garna left, Carina looked around. It was not a large room but a good open space and still so warm. There was also a little round window, rather like her own, with a lovely view of the silhouette of treetops against the deepening sky. She turned and could then see her own little fire glowing softly.

That night Carina dreamed of light. In her dreams, she passed a multitude of fires glowing. She was cold and pressed near them, but they gave no heat. She turned, desperate now in the cold, to see one little light standing away from the others. It hardly looked like a flicker of fire. Yet, as she went closer, the heat was amazing. It wrapped her round. Then the light grew, and standing behind the candle she could see a figure in a dark cloak. He turned slowly and there were tears in his eyes, even as he smiled. He was not only the water; he was the warmth and the light.

❧ Ancelin's Gift and Jasper's Tale

The next morning Carina awoke feeling much more refreshed for having actually been able to sleep a whole night in a real bed. One may not like having to go to bed. Yet, when you are without one, it is quite a different story. At any rate, everyone made her feel so at home. After breakfast Carina held Ruby and told Jasper a story as Garna finished clearing the table. Keegan and Aidan had already set out for the morning. She was nearly finished with her story when she heard rustling and movement. She turned to see Opal. Carina had thought that Opal was asleep, and that even when she was awake, that she would be very much unconscious of things. Yet, as Carina looked at her, there was some light still in her eyes. It was like the amber flecks of a fire dying, but still licking out for life. When Jasper heard her stirring, he ran over to her. He reached up and smoothed her hair. He wiped her face with a damp cloth and held her hand until she drifted off to sleep again. Then he returned to Carina's side as if nothing at all had happened. Garna returned, and Jasper wandered over to Opal's side. Then Carina began, "Garna, what do you know of Opal and her illness?"

"To tell the truth, I don't know too much about her at all. She must have come to the island not too long before the worst of the trouble began, or even after it, because I don't remember ever having seen her before the day she came to us; by then she was so sick already. She was never really able to tell me anything. She tried a few times, but she was just too weak. I'm not even sure how she managed to get here and knock at the door in the state she was in. Of course, I know there's growing old. There's something else too. It is almost more like she is heart sick or troubled. There is the look in her eyes and her restless slumber. Still, I couldn't leave her. I don't know what to do for her, but I couldn't leave her. Then a few days after she came, Aidan first caught sight of Jasper out in front of the house. He ran at first, and so we just left food and a blanket for him, and eventually he came to stay too. I don't know much about him either, except that he does seem to take a great interest in Opal. After they had both been here a few days, I asked Jasper if I might be allowed to give them both names. He seemed intrigued at the idea. I called him Jasper, and he agreed. Then I suggested several names for Opal, but he shook his head and motioned for me to step over by her bed. He pointed to the ring she wore, and so she has since been Opal. I wish I knew more. I wish there was something more we could do for Opal and for Jasper, but I wouldn't even know where to start."

"I'm sure you've started already by doing one of the best things possible."

"What would that be?"

"You've given them love and care and attention. You've given them a home when they were strangers to you. You've chosen them as family. What greater gift could you give?"

Garna smiled. A tear slipped down her cheek.

The next morning, after breakfast, Carina took a walk. She had not intended to wander so far, but the sound of the water wooed her, and she followed the stream down to the beach. She walked at the edge, and the waves were sliding in over the pebbles and over her feet. She looked down and noticed something bright floating in the water. It was a single pink petal. It washed up, then away, spinning on the tide.

Carina ran back to the cottage. "Garna, I have something, something I could try. I don't know if it would make any difference, but I know it wouldn't hurt. I have some herbs and medicine, from a friend who is one of the winged ones, and she is very knowledgeable about finding such things. She taught me a little about it." All of this came out breathlessly, and it took Garna a moment to decipher the words.

Then she smiled, "I don't know, but I suppose anything that you think might help. Yes. Well, what are we waiting for? What can I do?"

"Just a bowl of warm water would be good, and I'll find the rest."

Carina sprinkled the petals into a small white bowl by Opal's bed. She stirred the water gently, and they both watched as Opal breathed in more deeply and smiled a little. Then Carina took one of the other flowers, the kind that Ancelin had placed in her hair and gave it to Garna saying,

"Just place it in her hair." They sat together and watched over her. Garna began to hum a sweet melody. It reminded Carina of a lullaby her mother had once sung over her.

After a while of waiting, nothing more seemed to change with Opal's condition and slowly Garna went back to her work. Carina began to help her. Then Aidan came in and asked if he might take Carina along fishing instead. Garna insisted that she would be fine.

As they sat by the bank Aidan asked, "What were you doing in there with Opal? Is she worse?"

Then Carina explained about Ancelin. "She is one of the winged ones you know and very wise."

Aidan's expression changed, "Do you know much of the winged ones?"

Carina answered slowly, "Only the Eldress Altea, whom I told you about and Ancelin, of course. But I have heard many of Altea's stories about them. Why do you ask?"

"You don't know, then. I thought Garna might have told you. But then, I suppose not unless you had known to ask." Then he slowly stretched out, from under his cloak, two long dark wings, the color of fire burning, from a bright golden, to deepest red, rimmed in indigo.

Carina gasped, "You always hide them so well and I've no idea why!"

Aidan added, "You might if you knew more of the dangers of having such wings. But that is another story, and mine are not so good as yours," he paused. "Yet, will you tell me more about them? The other winged ones you know? Is that where you got the ribbon in your hair? It is of the kind, you know?"

"No, I did not realize that. But it was made my dearest friend, Ara."

"Is she another winged one? You did not mention her before."

"She is a winged one without wings."

"Then many would say she is fortunate," Aidan dropped these words heavily.

"Well, Ara would not. She longs for wings. Her grandmother was a graceful and strong woman who helped many through her gift, but Ara's mother did not have wings and always dreamed that Ara would. Ara would use her wings for good, but Ara already does so much good. She is so kind, full of insights, and she is awfully brave." Carina eyed Aidan to see how he would take her reply. He seemed to be thinking and this was enough for Carina.

In fact, Aidan wondered how brave this Ara must be to have impressed a friend who set out on a lone journey with an unknown end. He also began to think of his own brand of bravery and wondered if it would quite measure up to Carina's, or Ara's, or even the characters in the stories he had heard Carina tell. He listened, thinking of all of this, as Carina told him more of the winged ones she knew. A breeze went by. It ruffled his wings. Yet, he thought, it also felt good.

Later, they all had a good dinner of fresh fish and sat by the fire telling more stories. Carina was glad for their company. She was glad that her stories seemed to draw out Jasper, and that she had delighted Aidan with knowing other winged ones, but she had hoped she might be able to do something for Opal. That night, Carina came down in the quiet and sat by Opal's bed. She stirred the water and looked at Opal, thinking that there was something, just a little bit, in her face that reminded her of Altea. She was glad that Garna and the others had taken her in, and so she went back to bed thinking that at least if Opal had to be unwell, she was not alone.

The next morning Carina came downstairs to an empty house, completely. She noticed that Opal was gone and her bed made, and she was suddenly afraid. She ran outside. There she saw Opal standing in the sun and holding Jasper's hand. The others were standing quietly, a few steps behind them.

Opal was still weak, but so much improved and after a good breakfast and many "thank yous" she sat down to tell her story. She sat in Garna's chair by the fire with an aged quilt wrapped about her. Jasper sat at her feet and smiled at her with bright eyes.

"I came here to search. My own grandson disappeared two years ago. His parents had both passed on, and he was my treasure. I realized that a large ship had stopped just downriver, and the last place I'd seen him was by the dock. I got there just in time to see several men going on with large bags of supplies. Only then I saw the bags were moving and yelling and putting up a fight. I ran to the men, instead of going after help. They tied me to a tree and soon set sail. Eventually a neighbor came along, but by then the boat was gone. I looked everywhere for my boy, but couldn't find him. He's not the kind to run off. I know he was on that ship and I've been tracking it as well as I could since then. I came here because of the mines. I knew that some of the labor was, well not all hired. I thought he might have been here. In the process of looking for him, I meet other children who had been taken as slaves. I began working with a few others to get them out. I found Jasper tied up on the edge of one of the mines and left, even as I had been. I took him with me, and we were happy for a time.

"Then, I don't know, I just realized that everyone was leaving, and I didn't know where to go next. I went wandering down by some of the places near the mines, and I found a strange thing. I thought it was just another rock. It was a pearl, a black pearl, which shone and reflected and seemed to draw me into it. I picked it up and was surprised by how heavy it was. I was going to set it down. Instead, I just took it along and dropped it in my pocket. After a few days I grew so weak. It was a strange sickness. One afternoon we walked through the forest, and I was just unable to go on. I fell and the pearl rolled out of my pocket. Jasper saw it. He knew. He saw the pearl and was so frightened of it that I dared not keep it. But I could not let go of it in my mind, the fear, my grandson, the mines; it all took hold of me, and I could not grow well.

"This morning I woke up, I really woke up for the first time in a long time. I took in a deep breath, and I found there was life, still. There was Jasper standing over me, and I suddenly felt like getting up. It was he who led me here when I was too sick to do much else, and I am so proud of him," she finished, and smiled at him. It seemed to anyone who could have seen them, that they understood each other quite well, even with no words.

After this there was much celebrating and a great meal of fresh fish and fresh bread and then stories and songs to follow.

It was amazing how much Opal improved over the next few days. She seemed to grow younger and stronger each morning as she stood in the sun facing east holding Jasper's hand.

Of course, deep down, they knew it could not stay this way. It was Opal herself who brought it up one evening.

"How nice it's been here with all of you. I feel young again, but wiser for it. I can never tell you what your care means to me. I think of you as family. Yet, I can't help thinking my own grandson may still be alive, somewhere. Perhaps, even, he is looking for me, and then there's Jasper. Perhaps someone is looking for him. Then, perhaps, there are others too, looking for home. Carina, the ship that you described to me sounds much like the one that came to my village. I doubt there could be more than one just like it, and perhaps it may give me some clue."

"It does sound like the kind of thing that Malwell would do, and he was very secretive and harsh. I'm sure I saw some boys cleaning the ship one day, and I never saw them in town. It must be looked into. I just hate to think of you putting yourself in such danger."

"Yet," Opal continued, "I feel I must try, even as you must try?" she ventured.

"Yes, I suppose you have me there." Carina smiled at her. "And, at least if you are going, I can tell you what I know and those I know whom you may trust, if they are still all…well."

"I'm sure they are."

"But even so, the town is no longer the place it used to be, and I don't know what you might find there. It may be very dangerous for you."

"In this home I have been made well, and I have been loved," she added as she took Garna's hand. "I have little fear for myself, now. I have been given life again. Should I not spend it well?" she smiled.

"That and Jasper and I will be traveling with you of course," Aidan added. Then he said more softly, "I should like to travel with you, if I may, and be of help, if I can."

Garna had started to protest, but stopped short. Then she looked at Aidan, standing beside Keegan. He was growing up, after all. Opal nodded.

After their last dinner together, Garna, having little herself, gave freely of her stores. She called Carina into her kitchen and handed her a little purse. Carina opened it to find a key, silver and jeweled, and obviously old and valuable.

"Garna, this is lovely, but I can not accept it. You may need it still."

Garna seemed to answer her thoughts with a laugh and replied, "It is not a gift to barter, but to use. I know it seems strange and to tell the truth, I don't even know where it came from. I do know that it has been passed down in my family for many generations. We were once servants to a noble ruler, in a time when it was not a shame to be such a thing and this key, I believe, was a symbol of trust in that great house. Last night I dreamed of it and how it would unlock a long forgotten door, but the key was not in my hands. It was in yours. So I give it to you as the parting gift of a friend and as a symbol of trust in your journey. You have given us all such hope."

After all this, Carina knew she must go on. Aidan would soon be setting out with Opal and Jasper. Although she would miss them, she also felt that there was little more she could do now. It was time to go. But where?

Keegan had spoken of other islands. There could be hundreds. Opal had spoken of other islands too. But she had also made Carina wonder. Opal had questioned her about the stream by Aldwyn's house, the vines, and the way it seemed to appear, just at the right moment. "Perhaps," she had told Carina, "there is something to that. Perhaps, sometimes, you find yourself at the right place and, if not, perhaps the place will find you."

Opal's words seemed to make a sort of sense. Carina had not intended to come to this island, and yet here she had been able to bring Ancelin's help to Opal and here, too, she had made good friends and even been brought into this family. Perhaps there was something in that.

Now, Carina was about to set out again. It seemed to her that just when she was beginning to have something of a feel for a place, she always had to leave it. This often seems horrible at the time, but later on we have a different vision, and Carina had this shadowy thought too. After all, she had been well taken care of. She had found Aldwyn's home and then Keegan and Garna. They were just what she had needed at each step, and now she must take another.

Part 11

Golden Ship and Silver Dagger

In the hours alone again, Carina imagined what Garna's village must have looked like in its better days. She sat nibbling on one of Garna's seedcakes, thinking, "perhaps it was not so unlike my own." Then she imagined the changes, cruel slave drivers forcing the miners, some just children, to work day and night, forcing them into debt, taking their homes and, perhaps, even burning some, just for spite. Certainly, those living there had not intended for things to go so astray. But some were beaten down and broken, and others were driven, carried, or perhaps just looked away. And who had come to help? Certainly others must have known, must have heard? Why was it not ended sooner?

For want of comfort, Carina pulled out the pages of the book, and she ran her fingers over them with careful familiarity. She thought her eyes must be tired or tricked by the sea light. She found that a few of the words, that had been so faded, were, ever so slightly, clearer than before. She held them out and then brought them closer. It was true, however strange it seemed, that at least a few of the letters, the words, were actually unfading. She gazed in amazement. Then she heard the soft murmuring of the waters carrying her on.

The days lingered into a week, and with each new day, Carina hoped that the words would make sense, that she would see land, see anything, but there was only the water. At last she began to hope for even a passing ship, which could give her news, supplies, and maybe even shelter. It was the first glimmer of light, when, over the horizon, she thought she saw a faint shape, dark and moving against the waters. She was afraid to hope, but by noon it was in sight.

Then, as she looked at the ship again, something within her heart sank. It was not that she had seen the ship before, and yet the feeling it gave was familiar. There was a certain disappointment. She tried to reason with herself that there was no cause for it. A ship was what she had hoped for. It was a grand vessel too. As she looked, she could clearly discern the lines of ornate gold and the black and the blood red of the lower half of the ship. It was, in every way, calculated to be impressive. Even the sails were patterned with gold stitching, blazing in the sun. The ship sent out a row boat, with two men and one grandly dressed lady.

They approached her with smiles. "Poor thing," the lady gasped, hand on her heart, "It is a mercy that I am here now, to look after her. Just look at the poor child. She is a pretty one though, something in her eyes, reminds me of the sea."

"Yes, dear Lady," one of the men smiled at her. "Don't be too emotional. Don't upset yourself now," and he added under his breath, "There's hardly any need."

The other man rowed; he never spoke. He was poised for obedience and duty and yet his countenance belied a kind of weariness, bordering on annoyance, with those who seemed to be his masters. Carina could read in his face, what the others could not see. He thought them foolish.

They reached Carina and wanted to take her on board, but the third man would not allow it. He said to the other two, "She's not an emergency and now best to wait and see. We will tether her safe enough."

Another boat came, and the first begin its retreat as the woman cried demurely and looked over her shoulder at Carina, shaking her head all the time.

It was odd how they had looked at Carina and they had spoken about Carina. Yet, they never spoke to her, not even to ask her name, although she could hear them plainly. Carina mused, "They must think I have nothing worth saying to say. Either that or they suffer from a deplorable lack of curiosity. On neither account am I impressed." She sat with her chin on her hand and waited.

When at last they were gone, another boat approached. It was a simple rowboat. Yet, as it came closer, she could see lines of silver and deep blue on the oars and the craft itself. It seemed it did not really belong to this ship. Or, rather, this ship did not belong to it. There was only one rowing it and he spoke, finally, to Carina, "You are Carina? Carina…it means the keel. Your very name is of ships and stars. I am Selwyn and in, but not of this ship. We are not all past hope here," he smiled. It was a slowly spreading warm sort of smile. He continued, "Therefore, trust the provisions I give." He handed her a few parcels tied with string. As he gave her the last bundle he said, "Do not look so dismayed. Be encouraged. The light of the stars over the sea will shine for you, and when they come you will know what you must do. Perhaps you know already?" He held her gaze for a moment, and she could see in his gray eyes a deep hope. It was one that reflected in her soul as well. It was the sight of a sea, just beginning to clear after a storm, which she saw in his eyes. She looked out to the waters and back toward him. She believed she could trust him.

"Thank you. Thank you so much. Not just for these," she added as she touched the parcels, "but for your kind words." Without thinking, she reached out her hand across the waters.

He took it and held it while he spoke. "You are welcome. I wish that I could do more now, but perhaps the future will grant me another opportunity to be of service to you, My Lady. Farewell, Carina."

He left before she had a chance to ask any questions. However, some questions will bear the waiting. The sky and sea were mingling together into a silvery gray. A flock of gulls silhouetted in the last light circled, called, and moved on.

The first boat had tethered her boat to the ship. She must think what to do. Night had fallen, and out of the stillness she heard voices on deck. She listened. A man, very business-like, began, "We'll just leave it here for now, and in the morning, if all seems well, we'll take her on board." He checked the tether and continued, "The Lady Morwen was quite delighted with her, thinks she'll make a good lady in waiting when they get to that palace we're headed to. Although I'm still not sure what it is she sees in that new place, or this new ship. I always thought that Lady Morwen's fine *Blue Wasp* was a good and steady ship. I don't know why she wanted this new one."

"I've heard tell," replied the other, "that it's not the place, but the new ruler, that she's so interested in. Haven't you noticed how she's changed lately, all looks and appearances and hush, hush? I suppose she thinks that Malwell'll make her a good match. *Some* certainly seem to think so at least. I knew it was too good to last, the way things were before."

Morwen going to see Malwell? It was the Lady Morwen then. Carina had heard Altea speak of her as a kind ruler, but also as one who could be swayed by others. Then Carina thought of the lady in the boat, the strangeness in her eyes, and suddenly she remembered the black pearl on a string of lace entwined around her neck. Then she thought of Selwyn. She did not know what to think of this ship. However, one thing was clear; she could not stay and be taken back to Malwell.

Her boat was tied to the ship with a cord of twisted metal. As darkness came, Carina thought of the parcels and the one who brought them. She had thought they would be food, but then she remembered the last bundle and how it had been heavier than the others. She untied the string and paper and found not food, but a rondel dagger. The blade was just the length from her hand to the bend of her arm. As she removed it from its sheath and held it carefully, it shone a fair light. "That is what I shall call you, Fairlight," she whispered. The grip was of dark wood, inlaid with simple silver, but engraved with intricate patterns of waves and stars. The pommel too had these patterns engraved upon it. Then she could see that one edge of the blade was not smooth, but made of small, sharp, jagged teeth. She held it up to the light, and it reflected the shine of stars and moon and water. She knew what she must do. The tether soon snapped, and she waved goodbye in the moonlight. Only she was surprised to see someone on deck waving back. For a moment the fear of recapture surged through her. Then she thought of Selwyn, the hope in his eyes, his dark hair, his dark green cloak, waving in the wind. It must be him, and she decided she did trust him, whatever the appearance of the ship may have been.

It was harder letting go than she had thought. She had hoped the ship would mean rest and care, and she was leaving that chance. With Selwyn aboard, it could not be wholly bad and, yet, it was clear that this was not the ship for her. There was a certain freedom in cutting the tether and being done with the world, such as it was. She had given up a golden ship for a silver dagger. But even as she did so, she could sense the current moving with her. Softly but steadily, she began to move past.

🐚 A String of Islands

For two more days Carina drifted where the current took her. At last, she came in sight of what seemed to be a string of islands. She stopped to rest by night. As she continued on, one of the islands did as well. The next morning, it seemed the same dome of rock she had passed, had followed her. By morning's light she could see her "island" was the fair hill of a turtle's shell, patterned green and gray, like moss on stones. He turned round his head to her, and she gazed at his ancient eyes, green flecked with brown and gray. She wondered if he might be hungry. She remembered her provisions and ventured to offer him one of Ancelin's flowers. He accepted with a nod, and he hardly seemed dangerous now. For the next few days she traveled with her new companion, and guide, through the string of islands.

Although the first few islands were composed mostly of rocks and little else, the later islands seemed to be covered with grasses and wonderful, twisting, silvery green trees, and ripe little berries blossomed on vines at their feet. There she listened to the waters and watched the stars, the changes of the sky and air. There were birds too, lovely bright and singing. They were green and gold, blue and silver, and all sorts of other lovely colors, with streaming, curling tails. Her companion, Old Wise One, she called him, seemed to enjoy the sounds as well. He climbed up the pebbly beach of a larger island to bask in the sun with Carina. She told him of the old stories and he gazed far out to sea as if he knew them already and yet was pleased at the retelling.

When she went on, she hardly noticed that at last she was out of sight of any of the islands. Then, after two more days of calm waters, she found herself coming close to yet another sort of island. It was larger with winding, reaching trees and stranger still because she had not seen it the day before. Still, she knew from her friend, islands are not always as they appear. Old Wise One, with a rope griped in his jaws, pulled her in, past the rocks, and up onto the sandy shore. There she rested a day and wanted nothing more than the stillness.

Parting In and Out

The following day she pulled the boat further in and made it safe under some low growing shrubs and grasses. She gathered what was left of her provisions in Ancelin's basket. She put it on her back and fastened the dagger at her side, with the quiver across her shoulder, and her spear as a walking stick.

Old Wise One seemed to sense it was time to part. He had kept her safe through deep waters and rocky shores. He had guided her well. She gave him one last flower and a kiss upon the nose. He closed his eyes and seemed to smile. He watched her go. Then he turned toward the water as Carina headed inland to explore.

She had not walked more than an hour or so when she came upon the ruins of a once great house. She had been passing stones and bits of buildings and walls since the beach, but the forest had clearly invaded. The trees had climbed over walls, it seemed, with their great reaching roots. This was the first thing that seemed still whole. The gate was open, and so she thought to venture inside. She stood for a moment, with the sense that the trees were merely asleep, but very much alive.

After a moment of waiting and listening Carina walked on, only to realize that while the gate was open, the path beyond it had grown up much. She took Fairlight and had to clear the path, step by step, using her spear in the other hand to make her way. Sometimes, still, she was caught in the thorns of the undergrowth. Yet, it would have been impossible without the dagger and her spear.

Finally, she entered past a gate house and into a courtyard. There was a garden growing wild. There should have been lovely apple trees and pear trees along the wall and roses crossing the arches and covering the benches. There should have been statues and willows weeping for joy, but all was dry and withered. There were also dug out paths, dusty and winding through the garden. Carina knew them for dry stream beds and fountain basins. She walked on and yet found no way into the house itself. After circling a part of the large grounds, she found a stairway that lead up one of the walls. It went up and up, and then inside, and around turning, and going up and up. It was quite steep, and she was glad when she reached a landing. She passed through hallways and found always locked doors except for one, and in this way she spent the remainder of the day. At last she reached a high tower with a room full of windows. She was exhausted by this time and sat down to rest. When at last she stood and viewed the island, it was much larger than she had imagined and strangely golden brown, instead of green, in the dying light.

Carina fell asleep, then, exhausted, but woke in the night, thirsty. She had emptied her supply of water and seen no streams; yet, she half thought she could hear the sound of running water, somewhere. She tried to sleep again, but woke still thinking she heard something and feeling even thirstier than before. She searched the room, on hands and knees, crawling and then on tiptoe reaching, feeling over the stones and listening to the night and the sounds of coming water. She followed the sound up a tower that she had not seen before. She stumbled over the steps in the dimness and bruised and scratched her feet and legs and hands, more than a few times. At the end of the climb, there, at last, she found a basin for water and a spout. It was only a trickle, yet it was there. It was covered with dirt and debris and broken stones. She had not brought anything with her, and she was afraid that if she tried to return to the room for her dagger, she should not find the fountain room again. She began with her hands to clear the muck away, but all her effort made little difference, and at last she fell back into an exhausted sleep.

As the first light began to appear, she could still see only a small trickle and much of the old debris lingering, and she begin to notice her own cuts, bruises, and dirtiness. Yet, with the light, she finally saw her way clearly. She returned to the tower room for her things and then down to the dry garden. Leaving her basket, quiver, dagger, and spear on the bank, she ran empty handed into one of the dry streambeds. She put her ear to the ground and listened. Then she found a large rock and climbed upon it. She whispered, "Please." And as she waited, she fell asleep.

She woke suddenly. She thought she could hear the water, she thought, and at last with the sound of many waters, she was in it. She drank deeply. Then, submerged in the clear, cool spring, she dove and floated and swam and hardly noticed, at first, that everything around her was coming to life. The life was returning with the water.

At last she came out and sat on the bank, watching the roses bloom. Everything was so green and growing. There were arbors and fountains, all of which had been stone and dry before, now full of life and color and a beautiful sort of wild growing. She hardly noticed her cuts and bruises from the thorns of the path and her night of searching on the stairs. Then she seemed to feel something behind her, that sense that someone is watching.

She turned, and a figure in a silvery gray cloak stood behind her. He seemed to smile with the mirth of knowing a delightful secret that could soon be told. When he spoke, it was a warm sort of voice, not slow, but unhurried and not so much deep as full of depth, "Were you very thirsty, then?"

"Why yes, yes I was and I thought the water might never come."

"All you had to do was ask."

"Then, did you manage to clean out the fountain?"

"Yes, I did, my child. Now, will you come in? Perhaps you are hungry?"

"Yes. Thank you, Sir." Carina smiled, but paused.

"You have a question, my child?"

"Yes, it's just, there is no door. I looked and looked yesterday. I walked all around and then, finally, I found the steps into the towers, but not this part of the house. There was no door to be found."

"Ah, but today I am here with you, and that makes all the difference, you see." It was as if her eyes were opened, differently. There was a door where none had been before. A large wooden door arched at the top, made of dark wood with large black metal hinges. It was imposing. Yet, it stood open.

"Now enter in," he said as he held out his hand toward the room inside. Carina took a step and then paused on the threshold. It was a beautiful, spacious room with vaulted ceilings and light flickered from candles mounted on the walls as the fireplace glowed. Two chairs sat in front of it, and the table was ready. There were paintings on the walls and fresh flowers, not cut but growing everywhere. It was all light and warmth and loveliness.

"What then, don't you like it?"

"It's wonderful." She hesitated and then added, "But don't you see? I still drip with the river water and dirt and grass and leaves. I think even, perhaps, some blood. I am a mess and much too dirty to go into such a place."

Then he smiled, and then he laughed a warm, wonderful laugh. "You hardly need worry about all that, my child. My house has seen much worse, and besides you are my guest. We shall clean you up after you come inside. We could hardly stand on the doorstep and do it properly at any rate. After all, it is my house, and I have invited you. All you are asked to do is to accept." Carina smiled also, and her shame ebbed away. "Come in now, my child, and be at peace."

❧ In the Home at Last

S he sat by the fire to dry and was wrapped in a deep
blanket. In high-backed chairs by the fire they sat, and
she feasted on warm bread with butter and steaming soup. As
Carina held the bowl in both hands, she felt its very warmth
flowing through her. Then at last her host rose and bid her
rest, and so she fell into the most deep of slumbers, beyond
even dreams.

When she woke, for a moment, she thought Ancelin was
leaning over her. Rather, it was a lovely being with what
seemed wispy wings, tall and bright, like flames. She was
dressed in warm, golden colors and almost seemed to emanate
a light of her own or a flaming reflection of some light
brighter still. She smiled a small and thoughtful smile at
Carina and turned to tend the fire, and then she disappeared.

Her host returned with a basin and towels. "Ah, you've
seen Mercia, a tender of the flame. She will take good care of
you, my child." He came to Carina and smoothed her hair as
Calder had done, and she thought of her father. She was
surprised in the way the memory came to her. It was wrapped
warmly, in a smile, not in the coldness of tears as it had been.
Then he sat the basin and towels down at her feet. He dipped

the cloth into the water. It was warm and smelled sweetly of roses. He wiped her face, and then each hand, and at last each foot. He did this carefully, as if he were a servant, bound to do a good job, or a father, mindful of his daughter's hurts. Carina wanted to protest, but the words were lost in the awe.

Then he spoke, "Let's see about those wounds, from the branches and the stones, I gather? The path is not always to be an easy one, if you are to get where you most need to go." Carina held out her hands. The blood had dried across the cuts. He smiled and he touched her hands, wiping away the stains.

Finally, having finished, he looked up at her, saying, "You look as though you have another question to ask, child. What can it be?"

"I'm not sure I understand. Are you here always?"

"Yes, I am."

"But," Carina questioned, "I thought I saw you elsewhere. Were you there too?"

"Yes, I was. I am. I shall be. It is not an easy job," he added smiling.

"I'm still not sure I understand. There are so many things I don't understand. I suppose that is as it should be?"

"Of course, would you really have it any other way? Perhaps it will help if you think of your journey. Do you remember the guiding current, the voice of the waters?"

"Yes. Was it always you? The one I thought I had been seeking has been following me all along?" She mused on this.

"Not only following, but going before and walking along. There were many times when you did not see me and yet I watched over you the same."

Carina drew in a breath and sat trying to recall it all. "I thought I was looking for the beginning of a great magic spring, but you are also so like my father in many ways," she whispered at last, opening her eyes.

"Yes, child, I am. I am the spring, the first water flowing of The Source, beyond the Arvel Veil. I flow out, and yet I am received back. I have given myself a name that you may know and call on me, always. If only you will call out."

"Then, may I ask, what is this name?"

"Child, at last you ask plainly. You have been seeking what was lost and now you find it." He shook back the hood of his cloak and smiled, "I am your old friend, Elias."

Carina breathed in deeply even as she had tasted of the water, and she fell into his open arms. He embraced her as a father would a long lost child.

It was surprising to her, after all, that he should be there at that moment. It was finally not so surprising that he should be.

Carina was not sure how long she stayed there. It seemed to be forever and yet never long enough. She did not think of saying anything. It seemed, at that moment, rather unnecessary. Finally, she found a few simple words. "Forgive me. I did not believe."

Carina rested well that night, in her own little room, attended by Mercia, the beautiful flaming creature somewhat like Ancelin, but so different too and bright with light. She spoke to Carina and sang her to sleep. She reminded Carina of her mother, somehow, always watching over, smiling, and singing. It made Carina think that her mother would be pleased that if they were not together, at least Carina need not be alone, and she thought of her mother and smiled again. Then she thought of her father. Surely Elias must know of him too. She would ask him, she thought. How wonderful to be in such a home.

The Library
and Its Keeper

The next day Carina and Elias walked out into the garden, which overlooked the sea. She had so many questions, and he had so many answers, although he would not always tell her all that she wanted to hear. They laughed often. Throughout the day she saw others, beings with wings flying and others in the water. They shone silvery in the sea, splashing and singing. It was amazing, more real for being unreal. It was as if the rest of life had been but the shadow of things to come.

Then Elias took Carina to a part of the house, which she had not yet seen. It was a huge vaulted room with a deep balcony running all around. There were curved staircases in two diagonal corners and hallways heading off in four directions, from each wall of this large room, with more rooms still. There was a bright fireplace against one wall as well. All this Carina only noticed afterward, for there were also shelves and shelves of books. It was a grand, old library.

Then Carina looked up to see that there was a stained glass window and the room radiated its own hues of every color. The light danced in a fountain that bubbled in the center, the water reflecting the light, the light the water. Carina stood, wide eyed.

"Welcome to my library. I see you are pleased. Now, I want you to meet someone," Elias said. "This is Alpheus."

Before Carina's eyes, a tall, slender man appeared out of the fountain. He stood just on the edge for a moment. Then he stepped lightly to the ground and made a deep bow.

"Ah, Carina at last. We have long been expecting you," and he held out his hand, as he removed his hat. It was all quite courtly and would have made her nervous, had he not just appeared from a fountain.

Carina smiled and curtsied in answer to his greeting. Then she took his hand and it was, if one could imagine, like the touch of water held together but without the qualities of ice. Carina did not speak but looked at the man, his dark hair and green eyes, his suit of pale blues with top hat and tails; and then she looked at the fountain and then at Elias.

"Alpheus certainly does know how to make an entrance," Elias laughed. "Carina, he is one of those who live in the water, yes. He is also, if you will, the keeper of my library now and has been a good friend for many ages. He will be your tutor, while you are here.

"And," Carina interrupted politely, "how long am I to be here, may I ask?"

"For as long as it is needed, child," Elias answered with a smile.

"Then I feel I shall be here forever," she answered.

"Yes, perhaps you shall and in a way you are. Carina, all time here is but a moment and yet an age. While you are here, you are in what we call real time. It cannot be measured by the ticking of a clock. So, for this moment I shall leave you to your studies."

They sat by the fire and Carina asked, "What shall I call you, Sir?"

"You shall call me "Uncle Alpheus, my dear child."

"Thank you, Sir, I mean, Uncle Alpheus."

"Well, when shall we begin our lessons?"

"Now, if you please, Sir, Uncle Alpheus, I mean. Only, how is it that you come here, out of the water?"

"Child, in this house, all things are possible, but did you not know there are those of the sea who can walk on land as well?" He looked keenly at her, "Well, perhaps you did not. We may speak more of that in time. Now I shall show you around the library."

After they had walked upstairs and down and Carina had selected a few volumes, they returned to sit by the fountain. "Tell me, child, what do you know of the Battle of Lockwood Hill, as I suppose it would be called?"

So Carina began, "In those days a wise and beautiful Queen ruled with her wise and just husband, the King. They had a summer palace in a village near the North Mountains, where the clean water flowed into many deep lakes and on to the river. This is where she and her husband found one another. Here they also welcomed guests, winged ones from the forest and those from the sea. The villagers rejoiced at their coming. There were others, not so happy. Before the

King and Queen made a home there, it had been a hiding place for a great group of bandits. One came among them, stirring them to rebel and fight. He was not an ordinary thief, but a Twister of Tales, and he knew of the King and Queen and their wisdom and goodness. He knew they possessed a book of Truth, of stories flowing from The Source. He wanted to destroy this book, greatly, for he most of all wanted to destroy the truth, and he waged war to do it. But truth cannot be destroyed. The book of the three languages, old languages, those of the sea, the air, and the land was torn into three pieces. Yet a search would continue, and one day all could be put right again."

"Yes, child, good, and so that the book might be believed as true, and the line unbroken, the Queen took her necklace, a tear shaped jewel, a sign of her lineage and placed it with the book. The book you have is the language of the waters. You know something of it already, but I will teach you to understand more, My Lady."

A Glimpse of the Arvel Veil

Later Carina and Mercia were walking in the gardens overlooking the sea. Mercia's flaming light was not diminished out of doors, but her wispy flame-like wings undulated on the breeze. The wind grew soft, and she began to sing a low, sweet song. It reminded Carina of her home. Then they sat some time in silence. At last Mercia smiled and rose, saying, "I shall go for a while and leave you to your thoughts."

Carina wandered down to the shore. This was how Elias found her, and he stood back watching. Carina did not notice. She was looking out to sea. She saw something in the distance, growing, like a waterfall and a rainbow, and light and music all together. It came closer and stopped just past the breaking of the waves. The water there grew calm. She fixed her eyes on the sea. It was so beautiful, and it seemed so close. She walked out into the waters. Then she felt a hand lightly on her arm. It seemed to give a warning. "It is time to come back, child."

"What is it, Elias?" Carina asked this with her eyes still fixed on the sea.

"It is a glimpse of the Arvel Veil."

"It seems as though there is so much beyond it."

"Yes, there is. But it is not your time to cross it. There are other ways of learning what you need to know, for now. Come away?"

She turned toward him, and when she glanced back, the glimpse of the Arvel Veil was gone.

Back on shore, Elias began, "Tell me child, do you remember anything of your coming to the village?"

"Only what my parents told me of it. I came in the boat as a small child."

"But where did you come from before that? What sort of place and people?"

"I do not know, and I greatly wanted to know. I started out in that direction, I confess. Now, I find it matters more where I was headed. That has brought me to you."

Elias nodded. He seemed to be thinking on something. They continued to walk and made their way back to the home and up several stairways. There they came out into the sun on a rooftop garden, high above the ground and overlooking the house and the sea. Carina ran to the edge to see the glint of the waters. She turned around to see the spires and turrets, the only parts of the house higher than this garden. There were vines growing as well, on an arbor, around the edge, giving shade and sending sweet smells on the breeze. Three deep steps made a ring and lead her to the center of the garden. She noticed there was a beautiful mosaic of tiles covering the floor. She found that the pictures seemed to tell a story. Elias sat quietly in the arbor above as Carina followed the pictures. A fountain bubbled up in the center and streams of water flowed from it, winding through the images and over Carina's feet.

Then Elias began to tell a story, but he spoke in the language of the waters. Only, as he spoke, the images touched by the water seemed to move and come to life. They acted the story as Elias spoke. As Carina moved, a different part of the story came into focus. Yet, it was all there the whole time, all moving at the sound of Elias' voice; even the water followed his words. Carina thought she began to understand perhaps just a little.

She saw a village, near water, not unlike her own, and yet it was different, she could tell. Then the image shifted. She saw fighting, strange looking men and creatures. She saw a woman running through smoke and fire and a man fighting beyond her. He seemed to be fending off the battle as she ran. In the woman's arms was a child wrapped up, with something in its arms. The woman placed the bundle on the edge of the river. Quickly, she removed a tear shaped jewel from around her neck. She placed this with the child. Then she kissed the little baby and she spoke words, almost as if into the water. Then a beautiful lady, with long dark hair and bright green eyes rose up out of the water and took the child in her arms. She placed the child in a net on her back and swam down the stream at great speed. The lady looked after them for a moment. Then she turned and ran back into the village and chaos.

Then it all faded away; the village, the mountains. In its place, there was a lovely field with flowers and a stream, and through it walked the man and the lady, hand in hand. They were laughing and smiling. For just a moment they seemed to look at Carina, and then they turned to follow the stream and were gone.

"But who are they?"

"They are the King, Lord Gresham, and the Queen, Lady Adria, fighting for their people in the battle you call Lockwood Hill."

"Then is it the same? Does the child carry the jewel I carry?"

"Yes, it is the same."

Carina took from around her neck the silver circlet and held it out toward Elias. "Take it, please."

He held it in his hands. "What good care you have taken of it."

"It has needed little care. It has always had the light of the stars in it. Yet, if it is of the royal line you should have it."

"My child," he said, taking the necklace and knowing what it was for her to let go of it. "Thank you. Yet, my child, it has been given to you. If you give it to me, I hold it only as a gift. It belongs to you."

"How could that be?" Carina asked, "They are royalty. I imagine it was only placed with me, but never meant for me. Royalty? No. It is what I dreamed, but certainly cannot be what I am. Even if it is a sign of royalty, there would be no reason for me to wear it. I am no ruler."

Elias looked at her for a long moment. "Carina, how do you suppose one becomes a queen or a king?"

"You must start as a princess or a prince I imagine," answered Carina.

He smiled at her. "The child you saw went back to the waters and, in time, you came back to the land."

"You mean I am from the sea?"

"Always there is a reason. Look again." This time it seemed that Carina could see into the very depths of the sea. There were the people of the waters. Then something dimmed, the waters grew dark. She saw a woman and a man rushing away trying to out pace the tide of dark waters. Between them they carried a child. They headed up, toward the surface. Something seemed to hold back the darkness, just beyond them. The child was raised into the light and then the darkness covered the sea.

"Those were your parents. They saved you by giving you up to the land even as others saved their child by giving her to the sea. Such love, to give up one's only child."

"So that is why it is Uncle Alpheus, and that is why the language of the waters was always in me. That is why you are there with them and nonetheless here with me?"

"Things have been set in motion already. Many things have been tangled up, and it will take some undoing to make them right. I have made a way. Each must find it." Then he paused, "The necklace, yes, it is a sign, but it is not the reason for your royalty." He was quiet for some time, looking out at the waters. "Are you sure you will not keep the jewel?"

"No. It is beautiful, but somehow I feel I have no right to it. Please keep it."

"I will keep it, then. But I will keep it for you. And what of the pages you have carried so carefully, where are they?"

"They are here," and Carina removed the book from the pocket of her sash.

Elias took the book and held it carefully, running his fingers over the cover and the pages, almost as if it were alive. He smiled, but Carina could not discern the look of pain in his eyes too.

And so Carina spent her days between the library, the gardens, the great room, and the rooftop. Alpheus introduced her to many stories. The library seemed quite endless. She read histories, poetry, stories, riddles, plays, and anything she could find. She liked the words of the old songs, in the old language. Alpheus taught her to speak it and read it and sing some too. They sat by the fountain, and the water gave them music, like chimes ringing and strings playing. She could, by the hour, lie on pillows reading in the great library or out among the gardens. Alpheus was a great scholar and tutor, but he was not a hard task master and, of course, they never measured time.

She also grew to love the winged Mercia, who told her much of history and poetry and music but also watched over her with such care. She told Carina she had many students still to teach and many lessons still to learn, but for the time she was here to attend Carina.

Then there were the times with Elias. Each day, as Elias spoke, Carina seemed to understand a few more of the strange words. One day, she realized she had listened to a whole story; she had not only seen it in the water, she had understood his words.

"It is the story, isn't it? The one Altea told to me, but I didn't always understand?"

"Yes, daughter, it is, and it is the story that these pages hold too, along with many others. You are a part of the story, too, you see, and your part is just beginning. Carina, my daughter, I shall call you for now. One day, perhaps, you shall know another name. I have a task for you when you leave this place. A piece of the book was entrusted to you, but it is not whole. You understand, I do not ask you to make it whole. That must be my work. I only ask you to gather the scattered pieces, to protect them, until I ask. The pieces must be gathered, before it can be made whole."

What Comes of Learning

It was a lovely evening together, with dinner of fresh bread and cheeses and a cake too and the ripest strawberries and other such lovely things. They spoke of many things, and they laughed a great deal too. Alpheus was there and very merry and even Mercia joined in. Until, at last, all grew quiet, and then Elias seemed a little sad.

"Carina, how do you like it here?"

"Oh, so well! It's beautiful. I love Alpheus and the library, and Mercia and the hearth fires, the sea and the gardens, and I love listening to you. When you speak, it's not even as if you were talking to me. If you were talking to the me that most know, you would never say these things. Yet you do and they go deep into the something inside of me, touching my mind, my heart, my soul, the truer me, whom I don't even always know so well. And yet, perhaps, one day I will."

"My child, thank you," he spoke with a smile. His face spoke the rest, such bright eyes, and such love. He paused and his tone changed just a little. "And Carina, my child, how do you like it here?"

"But I just told you, it's wonderful. What do you mean?"

"Carina, do you suppose there are others who would like to know such a life as you have here?"

"Yes, I suppose, of course. The only thing that could make it better would be to have my family and friends here. Yes, there are many who would like such a life."

"And how will they know such a life?" He spoke these words with such a deep kindness and something else that Carina could not quite understand, mirth covered in grief.

"I, I don't know," Carina stammered. "I suppose I could go and try to find them and to tell them, and show them, only I don't know how much I could do alone?"

He smiled, and simply answered, "My beloved child, you are never alone."

The Edge of the Veil

E lias had said when she left, it would seem but a day had
passed from her landing. How could this be? Then why
did she need to go now? She looked with wonder at the part
of the book she had come with and a second section that
Alpheus had given her. It was bound like the other, but
written in characters wholly unknown. Alpheus told Carina
little of it, but he did admit that he had been keeping it safe
and that many had sacrificed much for it. He trusted Elias,
and he knew that Carina had learned so much. Therefore, he
let his piece of book go, knowing it was never truly his, but
only given unto his care. The books must yet be brought
together. This amazed Carina, and yet she could not see how
taking these pieces should do anyone any good.

The book, the pieces must be gathered. Others must
know. Why was this her work? Surely Elias could do it, or
Alpheus with his knowledge, or Mercia with her warmth,
even Ancelin with her wings. Any of them would be better for
this. So she was of a royal line? What was royal about her?
No. Nothing.

Carina thought over these things as she looked over the
pages. She found that she could understand much more of

her own piece, and yet the pages were still very much faded, worn, even stained and torn. She wondered how she would ever be able to really understand it or if she would find the third missing piece, which Elias had told her of. She had thought that finding him would be the end; that he would explain all and relieve her, as it were, of this burden. Instead she had more questions. It seemed she was beginning again.

She did know more, it was true, about the book, the language, even her past. But new questions grew each day, and one question haunted her still. What had really become of her father? She had asked Elias, and he had only told her that she must wait, still, for it was not yet finished. What could that mean?

At evening she walked down to the beach alone. She looked far out to sea, in the direction where she had seen the Arvel Veil. Then she thought of her parents. She thought of her father. Could he have crossed the Arvel Veil already?

If only she could see it again, once more, she thought, then, perhaps, she would be ready to leave. Would she ever be ready to leave? At least she would know what happened to her father. But Elias had said it was not her time to cross the Veil. Well, she would not cross, no. But if she could get closer, she thought, perhaps she could get a better glimpse and then know. She hesitated for a moment. Perhaps she was not meant to know. If Elias had not answered her questions, was it not better to listen to him? Yet, he had not told her that she could not go into the waters, and she was a strong swimmer. If she swam and the Veil appeared, what was the harm? Yes, she would try. She gave one longing look back to Elias' house. Somehow she felt it was suddenly very far away.

She dove in and headed in the direction of the Arvel Veil. She thought she caught a glimpse of it; then, when she arrived, it seemed farther away. Although she was a strong swimmer, at last she knew she could not reach it alone. By then she was far out to sea. She turned toward the shore, but now it was so far. She cried out to Elias and all seemed to fade.

Then there was light. The current took her on a strange journey. It buoyed her up and she floated in it. She wound around streams she could not place, through beautiful forests and fields of flowers. It was as though the water carried her just through them. She never lacked for good fresh fruits to eat, or even water, for the very stream was sweet. The animals came out of the forests and glades, vales and rivulets to meet her. They ate from her hand and gave her quiet company, sometimes even walking along beside her for awhile. She found that she did not feel lonely there, nor could she stay though she very much wished she might return someday. For now, the current carried her on.

Then, as if waking from a dream, she sat up on a sandy bank; it was not a shore she knew. She looked around, puzzled. Her own little boat was there, stocked with all of her belongings, provisions, and even the books. She stepped in and set off again. At last she came through a forest, and the current took her down a smaller branch of the stream. These waters ran into another stream, and after a day's travel, she knew where she was. She was at the town just upstream of her own. She had not crossed the Arvel Veil. She had been close to its very edge, and Elias had brought her back. She had followed the current and yet come from a place close to The Source. Elias had rescued her and helped her on her way.

🍂 Strange Reunion

S he knew that even at night she would be a likely target on the river. She had to think again of the kind of place her town had become. It was hard to transition. So she pulled ashore in a wooded area, hid the boat as best she could, gathered what she needed and began a wary walk. She dared not go openly into the village, but stayed on the outskirts for several hours, observing. She saw a few of Malwell's men and steered clear. She went as close as she dared to some of the homes, but found them empty. She heard no news and saw no familiar faces. At last she grew very homesick. She made for her own home. She reached it, but found it empty. Everything was still, yet unsettled. It was dusty and cold. They were not simply out; they were gone, but where? She had seen no one. Where was she to go? As she continued to gaze through the window she saw a light moving about inside. Through the front door came Malwell himself. Although disguised in a long dark robe and hat; she felt at once his presence. She watched him carefully, and he sat down near the window. It was still dark outside and she stood, hardly daring to breathe. Then he pulled from a box a glowing orb, like a large pearl, but pulsating, almost as if alive. It held his attention and he looked into it, concentrating upon it. Then he jerked suddenly and looked about.

Carina turned and ran away. As she crossed the garden, he met her at the gate. He perceived her fright, but was otherwise impatient. Indeed, he almost seemed relieved to see her. He mumbled the words, "vagrants" with a certain amount of tired disgust. Then, with exaggerated gestures of the face and arms, he motioned for her to be quiet and to follow him. She hesitated, but with a smooth gesture, he made visible the hilt of a sword and so she followed. He looked around again, and then with a sigh, he led her away from her home. It was just growing into dusk and everything seemed still. At the edge of the water he motioned her into a boat and handed her a blindfold. All the time he said nothing to her. He mumbled a few words to himself as if Carina were not even there, as if she were merely a stray dog or cat.

It seemed he crossed and recrossed the river, but at last he landed and led her up a steep path. Then it grew even darker and muted, the sounds snuffed out with the heaviness of the night, and she sensed a change in the space around her. Finally, he started to speak, "You may remove the..." Then with another sigh, he untied the blindfold and put it again into his pocket. He led her down a hall with many doors on either side. He paused at one and checked the lock, then continued on. He led her to another dark room, looked up and down the hallway, then pushed her forward and closed the door.

Carina looked around at the dark room. There was a small fire glowing in the middle and beyond that, only shapes. Then one of the shapes in the corner began to move. Was it an animal? A guard? And then it advanced slowly, awkwardly and then in the light of the fire she could see a person, a woman, limping toward her.

Her clothes were worn but her eyes seemed very bright, especially in the dim light. She crossed the space and approached Carina. A few others figures begin to stir. Carina simply stood.

The lady spoke, "Oh child, have they hurt you? Are you well? You are frightened I suppose. You will find no more harm here from us. Come, come," she motioned to the others. Then as she caught a glimpse of Carina's face in the firelight, she gasped, "Can it be, my star, my Carina? Speak child, tell me who you are."

Carina answered with one word, "Mother?"

After this, there was a very happy prison reunion. They sat together for a long time, just quietly. Late into the night Carina shared her story. When her mother had heard all, she looked at Carina and held her face in her hands, "My child you mean we were chosen for you and you for us? What a blessed gift you are. I think, still, if I may say, you must not tell this secret to any other. It is too dangerous in such a time, my child. But one day—"

"Mother, I would hardly try to stand and proclaim myself queen. I am no queen, I know."

"Rather, it seems you are. Even if you proclaim it not, you have always been. Yet," the joy left her voice, "If Malwell knew—your life, my child."

"I understand. I do not intend to proclaim it, but not for fear of Malwell." Then her tone softened and she added, "I shall always be content as your daughter."

"And am I not glad to hear it? Yet, my child, my love, you are a queen."

"Then, how unfit I am to be what I am." She whispered this to herself.

In the following days, Carina found many of her friends. She discovered that they were rather tired and hungry, but generally left alone, except every day or so when a guard brought food. It took hours, even days, for Carina to tell her story and for the others to tell theirs. At last it was done and they were all very glad to see her, though not in such circumstances. She tried to explain about Elias and some were very interested. Others thought it all just another story. Some even complained, saying, "If he is who you say, why doesn't he come and help us? Why does he leave us to suffer?" But even so, many listened to her stories over and over again.

They were also able to tell her that not too long after she left, Malwell had begun to sway the council and the village with wonderful, wild tales and extravagant gifts. Then he brought in soldiers and made them citizens, giving them property, protection, and prestige, and those who disagreed were offered "free passage up river to a new settlement." Of course where most eventually found themselves was prison.

Some had managed to escape and were said to be hiding in the forests. Others, a few, had managed to hold on to their places in the village, quietly biding their time and some, even as Carina had, seemed to have disappeared altogether. Ancelin had made her promised trip to the village and then several more. It was thought she and Aldwyn had helped some to escape. With those who were left, Malwell had called for a council meeting, without the voice of Calder and several of the town's people, he gained their vote and they pronounced him king. From there, of course, it only grew worse. He completed the bridge on the river and all ships that came through had to have his permission. Fewer and fewer came, unless they were on his business. It had further alienated the village. He had also brought in many new "workers" who were actually little more than slaves and, oddly enough, kept trying to run away.

There were a few things in all of this to be thankful for. One was that, even at great danger, Altea had stayed for the vote, but escaped shortly after. In doing so, she had a fairly good idea of who could be trusted now. Ancelin had also been seen, again, in the village a few days after the council meeting. It seemed Ara and her father had made it out of the village or, at least, were not in this prison. This Carina was very glad to hear and the thought that Ara and her father were perhaps still free and somewhere with Altea and the others, even now, gave her great hope.

Although her dagger had been taken, Carina had made it this far with Ancelin's basket of herbs, which had not been seen as a danger and the two pieces of the book in her sash pocket, which had not been seen. She produced these and gave aid to the sick and told them the stories she knew. It revived them in many ways and so, although they suffered, they were together. It was also with a certain relief that Carina remembered how she had given her spear, bearing the names of Calder, Eldoris, and Carina, to Alpheus as a gift. He had said, "A token of remembrance, borrowed, until we meet again."

Carina had found a place in the back of the room among loose stones where roots were growing in. She hid the books there. She took them out only for short intervals and at night. Carina read what she could and tried to tell the others what she remembered. She admitted she did not understand it all, but she did not tell them how it pained her. She took much care in the hiding of the books. At night she slept near the wall where she could hear a trickle of water running down the walls. She tried to remember all that Elias had said, but there were still so many questions and the thought of the Arvel Veil sometimes came to her. It swept over with tears and the thought of how she had left the House of Elias.

In the following days they realized that although Malwell himself had brought Carina to the prison fortress, he clearly must not have recognized her. Even her mother had not in the darkness, at first, and it did seem that somehow Carina had changed. The others also told her that it was unusual for Malwell to bring in a prisoner as it was generally reserved for the work of his guards. When Carina had explained his disguise and manner, they wondered what it could mean. They did not know, but they agreed that it was strange, even for Malwell.

As the days wore on there were rumors from the guards that some of the prisoners were to be moved. Carina was not sure whether to be glad or anxious. She was concerned that she might be separated from her mother. She was concerned for the books. She was also desperate to get out. She wanted to see the sky and feel the wind and, especially, to hear the water. "If only I could get to the water," she had often whispered, "perhaps I would understand, perhaps." And so she dreamed of the waters and the voice of Elias spoke quietly, even there.

Stories Found

The story Alpheus had told her of the book came back to her in dreams. Long years ago Elias had helped some to write their stories, their stories of The Source, the Sceop, so that a written record could be kept and passed on. For The Source flowed from a place beyond the Arvel Veil. For some time they and their children kept the books well and shared them and many copies were written. Then some grew prideful and began to think that only certain people were worthy of reading the stories at all. They sought to keep the book from being translated. Some languages were not worthy of it, they had said. In their great desire to preserve, they hoarded the stories and then forgot what they were really about. Although this was a great sorrow for many, it was a great advantage for their enemies, A Twister of Tales and his followers. They wanted to use the truth for their own gain and glory and bent it greatly to do so. Many copies were destroyed, but some had survived and one, the first one, was kept at much peril to many lives. It was, in fact, in this way that it had been separated. The truth, written in the languages of the waters, of the air, and of the soil, which had once been all together, was rent and scattered. Carina had held the book of the waters since her childhood and she had been given the one of the winged ones, which had come at great cost to Alpheus. There was yet one missing.

However, Alpheus had said there was truth still whole as long as there was Elias, for he was the very truth of the stories himself and the first spring to flow from The Source. Uncle Alpheus had told her many things she could not always comprehend. Yet, as she held the books, as she saw Elias, as she listened to the waters, they all seemed to say the same thing, in different ways. Perhaps this was what Alpheus had meant.

She awoke and, instead of the quiet restless waking, the prisoners were called with more noise than usual. Several guards came in and began forming the prisoners into groups. They were to go work in the fishing boats, they were told. At first, the guard walked past Carina and Eldoris. On a second pass the guard looked at Carina and motioned for her to move away from her mother. She hesitated and her mother reached for her. The guard brandished the handle of the whip he carried and threatened to strike Eldoris. She caught his eye, held his gaze, and stood firm. It was something like the look Carina had seen Altea give an impudent student who dared to be disrespectful. He hesitated and turned away. It seemed Eldoris had changed in some way too. Carina reluctantly followed him thinking on this.

She was soon mending nets out by the water and it was, in its own way, a relief from the enclosure of the cell. She was concerned for her mother, and the work reminded her of her father and of the way in which she had left Elias. Yet, the sounds of the waters wrapped around her more and more and the books were yet safe.

At the end of day she was taken, along with the others, back to the cell. That night she took the two parts of the book in her hands. She held them together. Then she turned through the pages, slowly, her fingers barely gliding along the edges and then down the spine as she closed them again. She turned them over in her hands once more and hid them away again as best she could. Carina felt it the best plan, although she knew it could still be risky. Her main hope was that even if the books were found, they would simply be dismissed, as no one knew the languages they contained. For the next few days, her routine remained the same. At the end of the week one of the head guards came to oversee the work.

"His Majesty Malwell requires servants to clean and clear the old residence," the guard told one of the others "and I have come to see if I can find a few who may do."

And so Carina's mother went, not to the new house, but to the old castle ruins where things were being shipped and stored. Their plan seemed not to make the old castle livable for Malwell, but to use the lower rooms as storage. Eldoris was not told why. She was only assigned to move items, clean, sort and move more things. She was gone for days at a time while working there. She worked so well, one of the guards thought that she might do for service in the new house.

In fact, she was sent to help collect things from Malwell's own apartments in the fortress in town, which were to be moved to his new and grander apartments, constructed near the city's center. She was given a list of things to find, care for, and carry over and then told to sort and pack the rest. It took her several days of going through rooms and rooms. She found many strange things, but at the end of each day, the guards made sure she had taken nothing with her. Not that anything of much value seemed to have been left. Malwell had already taken many things, and then guards had been through the rooms as well. So trustworthy she was and because she did work so well and was pleasant, the guards worried her little. There was something in her face that looked so calm and kind and yet inwardly fierce. Although she certainly was not old, they gave her a sort of respect or at least indifference.

At the end of one especially long day, Eldoris was sorting through a pile of books and papers left by the fireplace. The guard had told her they were to be burned, but she had pleaded to be allowed to sort them first. The guard sneered and said, "Well, if it's extra work you like, I suppose it'd be cruel of me to deny it to you." So Eldoris worked long into the evening. At the bottom of the pile she came across an unassuming little book, but as she turned it over, something in her jumped. It looked like one of Altea's books. She thought of the library and of all the stories that were being lost. Then another guard came in and looked at her. She returned his gaze, kindly. He appeared rather old and worn from time on the seas or perhaps his own burdens.

"So you like to read then?"

"Oh yes, but of course, and even more so my daughter. She loves stories, books, and would cry I'm sure to think of them going into the fire, especially when there aren't really books for the asking, in these times," and her voice trailed off and the light left her face.

"Well, I never learned myself; had a daughter once though, and she used to read to me a bit now and then. But that was all in a different life. Well, now, I guess it wouldn't hurt, especially seeing as how they were going to be burned, if you took just a few. Of course, I'll take no responsibility if you get caught with them, mind you, but I'll also look the other way as you go," he added with a smile.

🎐 Stories Lost

E ldoris returned that day and tried to hide her joy over the books until late in the stillness of night. She woke Carina, as tired as they both were, and pulled her away from the others. She waited as she woke and handed her the few books she had saved.

Carina, at last awake, went to find the other two books. She felt for the stone and discovered it was already loose. Her breathing quickened. She felt again. She overturned the stone. Nothing was there. She looked again and again. Her mother came and wrapped her arms around her. Her heart was breaking; the two pieces of the book were gone.

Carina and Eldoris decided their best plan was to try to remain calm and draw no unwanted attention. As quietly as possible, they scoured the prison and when others awoke they began to question them as openly as they dared. For two days, there was nothing. On the third, one of the other prisoners, Larsen, came to them, slowly.

"I, I just wanted to look. I've been here so long. I just wanted to see something besides these walls. I was digging and I found the book. I didn't, couldn't read it, but just the same I felt something just to hold it and I thought, when I opened it, just for a second, I heard a voice, a voice like waters and wind and then it faded away. So I took it, just to look at it, but, well, the guards came in and I tried, I tried to hide it but one saw, saw it, and he, he did take it. I tried to hold on I did, but," he left off there biting his lip.

"You shouldn't have taken it," began Carina. But her mother stopped her. It was only then that Carina saw the bruises on his downcast face.

"Now, now," spoke Eldoris, "You could have asked one of us. But, it has been done, and it could have just as easily been one of us. There is nothing to be done with worrying over it. We must think how to trace it, and you must help. You will be the most important in this. Do you know which of the guards may have it or how he reacted to it?"

"Well, there was one guard. He seemed disappointed with it, like it wasn't much to him after all the…after all."

"Good," replied Eldoris. "It is well that he seemed not so happy. Perhaps, even, it is somewhere lying about. I am certain we will find it. Is there anything else you remember?"

"Well, there was the first guard who seemed disappointed. He only took the one book. I hid the other behind me. Then there was another guard. He came in to see what the commotion was about. He dismissed the first guard and started to walk away. Only then he came back, and that's when he found the other book. I don't think he knew there were two. He asked me a few questions about it. I told him I found it digging about the walls, which is true. Only he thought I meant digging about the walls of the old castle, I think, where I'd been working, putting the upper rooms to rights in the old castle. He reminded me I was to report any findings to the guard, immediately."

"And you didn't correct him?"

"No, no. He asked many questions about where I had been working, you see, and I told him, and so that was his own idea, his own idea. I didn't lie, you see, I didn't."

"Yes, child, I see, and I believe you."

Carina believed him too. Yet, the books were gone. What else mattered?

The next day, when Eldoris was sent to the ruins to work, she was met by the guard who had helped her, Delwin. As she worked, he shouted orders to those nearby. Then he sent those who were working near her on an errand. He made certain the halls were quiet. Then he handed her a parcel, bound in old leather and cord. "I got this off of one of the prison guards. I told him I was in charge of burning the books and he laughed and gave it up as worthless. But I warn you, it could have been worse, if he had not been such a fool. Mawell sorts through the books too. Those burned are only his cast offs. He is looking for something."

Eldoris peeled back just a corner of the wrapping and breathed a gracious sigh. "Thank you. Thank you. You do not know. You do not know. This most of all is a precious treasure. But what shall we do then? It is my daughter's legacy and her fate to protect them."

Delwin looked puzzled by this, "I don't know of all that, but don't upset yourself now. I have been thinking, of what you spoke, before. Perhaps it will not always be this way, and perhaps someone will be wanting these stories and histories. I must be about burning something and I have fed the fire with leaves these past days, but not of books. I think this old castle will be a perfect hiding place. They will think them burned, and these lower apartments will be empty or at the most storage I gather. If I have gained the trust of you and your daughter, I hope I shall be more honorable by and by, and I want to make this my start. Shall we work on hiding these books?"

The man reminded Eldoris of her own father. Yet, at that moment, he looked more like a timid but excited child, standing on the edge of the water waiting to take his first dive.

"Yes," she answered, "You will bring them here to burn and we will hide them instead."

The next night Eldoris was returned to the prison and she gave the parcel to Carina, whose joy and relief was suddenly checked, "But mother, there is only one book in here. What am I to do?"

The New Estate

The next day Eldoris received word from Delwin that while one guard had supposed the book quite worthless, the other guard was identified as Lieutenant Nuewell. He had been sometime in the confidences of Malwell; yet, more recently, he had fallen out of favor. Delwin could not say whether this Nuewell might be trying to get back into the good graces of the Captain or whether he had some other plan. Still, they hoped it could all be sorted out and the book would soon be dismissed and sent to Delwin, "to burn." Only, it did not come. Could it be that it was somewhere in Malwell's possession? It seemed at last likely. Carina knew what she must do. But how would she get into the New Estate?

This problem, at least, was soon enough solved. It followed that Malwell, desiring to show off his supposed kingdom, planned a grand ball, inviting many lords and ladies and notable figures from the surrounding cities. It was for this purpose that Carina was taken from fishing to serve in the New Estate of Malwell, as it was called. She was not exactly happy about this, but she took comfort in the thought that she might continue the search for the missing book. Everyone who could be trusted was also about this. She also found something else to take comfort in. On her second day she was assigned to the charge of another servant, one Ara, and it was a most joyous scene, although they tried not to let on that they knew one another, so as not to be separated. As soon as they were alone, there were many hugs and tears and stories to be shared. Ara's father, as far as she knew, was serving, against his will, at an outpost down river, in the marshes, but was safe.

Something else strange came to light. Ara asked Carina, "Did you know of any other servants who were to come?"

"No, why?"

"They told me that I should have a hard time with the charge I would be given because she was one of those strange looking foreigners, who did not speak the language. Do they think that of you?"

"I don't know? I don't suppose they would have heard me speak much and the night I was brought in by him, he did act so strangely. He didn't seem to recognize me. He rarely spoke, but made motions, and I never replied. Yes, yes, perhaps they do."

"Then he doesn't know it is you, or that you are even here!"

"And…he doesn't know that I understand what they say."

"Have they asked you for your name?"

"No, why?"

"You must change it. It will be safer if they don't find out who you are and if they think you don't understand. They often say things, hints of things, when I'm about, but then they notice and stop, if they thought you didn't know…"

"Then, they might go on speaking," Carina finished.

"But what will you tell them your name is?"

"I have something in mind."

"But you must remember to pretend that you don't understand."

"I think I can manage pretending; it may even prove to be a bit interesting."

"Oh, but you must be careful." Ara suddenly seemed worried. "This is no game we play. It is not a part in a story."

"Rather it is, Ara. It is our story. But I do understand. I will try to be cautious, and if not for my sake, then for yours."

So days of hard work, cleaning, polishing, and moving one thing from here to there and back again, followed. Ara was in charge of Carina, known as Adria, one from an island, and this worked well to keep them together. However, Madame Pompadu was in charge of all the household servants. She kept them busy preparing for the grand ball, while she dallied with the guards, and fed herself sweets from the kitchen. There, the chef was supposedly, "trying new things that must be tested before the banquet." Due to this, perhaps, and trying to pass the real work off to others, Madame was a somewhat round sort of person, and she kept a great quantity of hair piled upon her head with ribbons and beads. Yet, she did hold a certain sway, having the keys to many rooms and claiming the run of the house when the "Captain was to be at sea," as she said. She also seemed, perhaps due to the large ring of keys, to somehow or other overhear many things and, as she liked the attention, she also had a way of letting things slip once in a while, for the right price. With all of the preparations, Madame was bustling around a good deal more. So Carina tried hard to listen for information, and as often as she could she wandered off into other areas of the estate. Whenever she was caught "out of place" she simply claimed ignorance and begged for mercy in her broken speech. She was very convincing in this.

One afternoon she and Ara were assigned to dust the hall tables and mirrors. They worked quickly and kept going, farther and farther up the hall and then to the second floor. There, in a parlor, she heard several voices. She stood by the hinge of the doorway and listened.

"'Now Nuewell,' he said to me, you know how he is, 'Now Nuewell, what's that there?'

'Begging you pardon, Captain,' I said, 'It's a book I believe.'

'Very amusing, Nuewell,' he answered, and 'what are you doing with it? You cannot be reading it to be sure.'

'No Captain, no indeed, I leave that to others, better fit for it. I was taking this one to the fires, of course.'"

"Then he said, 'Well, I believe I will just take a look, first, my good man.' I tried to reason with him and to say there was no need for him to add to his work, but he would not have it. He gave me a bit of gold and sent me off. Well, that's all I know of it and whether or not it is the one he has been looking for, I do not know. I do know when I questioned the prisoner about it, all he would say is that he found it in the ground, under some rocks, just found it."

"But what of this book? Why did you want it?"

"I mainly want it as I know the Captain also wanted it. He's been searching these many days through old books and older books. And this one was a right strange one indeed. But it's easy enough if I want to get my hands on it again. I know right where it will be, in his apartments. There's even a trap door beyond a trap door. That's the only reason the Captain still treats me so well, and I can treat him so ill. I know too much, and he knows it too. But, then, if the book goes missing I shall be a suspect. So I am biding my time to see what else comes."

"And so you think the Captain thinks it came from the old castle, and now you want to go there, looking for treasure too?"

"Yes. If the Captain's set on finding something, it must be valuable, and maybe I'd like to find it first."

"I don't much like the old place. There's tales of a flying sort of ghost who appears and vanishes right out of the air."

Nuewell laughed, "You are as bad as those peasants."

"Well, best to be safe now, and what do you think is so valuable there anyway?"

"There is the legend that says along with the old book there is a treasure of some sort."

"I thought you didn't believe in those sorts of old fool's tales?"

"No, of course I do not. But I do believe in treasure."

Then they turned toward the window laughing, and she heard steps in the hall. Another guard was coming toward the room, and she hurried off to tell Ara the news.

Malwell was searching, and he had one book. If the book was there, somewhere, they could find it, especially if Malwell was preoccupied with finding something else. For the next few days, Carina tried to get away. As the ball approached, everyone only grew busier and her hopes were postponed again.

When the night of the grand ball arrived at last, Carina, Ara, and the others, who might be seen by the guests, were given new uniforms, of the crispest kind. They were long, dimly red dresses, with long black aprons, trimmed in intricate black lace and tied with a ribbon at the neck. Carina felt nearly choked by it, and yet all together, they made a stunning string of "black pearls" as they were called. Carina, herself, had nearly missed all of this and been ordered to the kitchen, by virtue of her supposed lack of understanding of the language. She had in fact rather hoped for this. She did not want to see or be seen by Malwell. They were one short, and so she was ordered by Madame Pompadu to serve at the grand dinner and told to "remember her place."

The Grand Ball

The New Estate was polished and burnished in gold. Everything seemed to ring with it. The ballroom was glaring and too grand. It was nothing like the silver and clear brightness of the sky that Altea had described the old castle to have been like. Carina thought of Altea, and her mother and father, and wished that they might have all lived in that other time in Veradis Kel when it was as it should be. Even now Carina's mother described it as beautiful.

She was interrupted by Ara's pointing out places at the table in the hall. Madame Pompadu came sweeping in for one last check. She rattled off a guest list to which Carina was only half listening, "...The Lord Lucrue and Lady Lucrue, the Misses Vaderhaults, the Lord Gaspert, the Lady Morwen, Baron VonButiff, Lieutenant and Lady Smudgitt..." and on it went.

At last the guests arrived, were taken care of, and finally came down to dinner. They were all "at the height of fashion," as Madame said. If this was its height, Carina and Ara agreed they should hate to see its lowest point.

For now, Carina and Ara and the others were too busy taking things to and from the kitchen and waiting on the guests to think of anything else. Once they moved into the ballroom Carina thought she could return to the kitchen. Instead, she was stationed in the ballroom, with a tray of glasses, which was ever being taken from and just as soon refilled by another servant.

Carina tried to be quiet and keep her head down. As the music stopped, one of the guards announced that they were to be favored with a few songs from a musician in the company of Lady Morwen. Then someone, standing nearly beside her, smiled and bowed slightly to the room. He glanced at her and smiled before approaching the front of the hall. She recognized him at once. It was Selwyn. As he began, Carina could not help but lift her head to listen. The songs were beautiful and the room stood almost silent. It was a moment of peace, real peace, such as she had not seen in this house. If she would have glanced at Malwell, she would have seen him shudder.

It was not long after this that Captain Malwell, with a tall and lovely lady on his arm approached Carina. She bowed, hoping her attempt at not being recognized would pass for shyness and awe. The lady on his arm, taken by this, only smiled the more and lifted Carina's head to look at her fully. "Ah, a pretty one, and so humble and so, why, so strangely familiar. If I didn't know better, I'd be sure that I had come across this face before and yet," she sighed, and then to Malwell she added, "Where is she from?"

"Oh, why, she came to us from far away hearing of the prosperity of our land, and you see how happy she is, only you mustn't ask her," he added quickly. "She doesn't speak the language yet, but of course I'm overseeing her education personally."

"How do you have the time? You are such a committed leader to these poor people. Only she does look so familiar," and then looking at Carina once more, she added, "It's a shame you don't speak the language. Ah, but the Lady Morwen gives you her favor anyway, and perhaps before the night is through, I shall remember where it was I have seen such a face before."

Only Carina remembered first. But perhaps it would be of no consequence, perhaps.

The Lady Morwen

The Lady Morwen was to be a guest of the Captain's for a fortnight at least. Carina was called by Madame to be Morwen's lady in waiting at the New Estate. It was true that the Lady Morwen had many servants of her own, but none she liked so well as Carina, or Adria, especially as Morwen was a stranger in these parts too.

Carina found the Lady Morwen to be kind and rather good hearted, and yet it seemed she had also been blinded to Malwell's true intent and nature. She wondered what it might take to make Morwen see. She also found the Lady Morwen spoke to her of many things, even though she admitted that she knew Carina could not understand all of it. "Only," she said a few days later, "you really ought to understand something, with Captain Malwell overseeing your education personally." From that moment forward she was obsessed with doing what she could to alleviate some of the Captain's work by tutoring Carina herself. At first Carina had, perhaps, a bit too much fun at her expense, with her mispronounced words and phrases. Yet, as she saw Morwen's determination, she left off with the games and earnestly listened to all she had to say. After a lesson one afternoon Morwen told her, "Adria,

I do believe you know much more than you seem to know. There is a mystery about you, though." Carina only gave a puzzled look.

"I would like to do something to help you, Adria."

For a moment Carina thought about trying to tell Morwen who she really was. But would she understand? How loyal was Morwen to Malwell? Carina could not be sure.

"Adria, dear, is there not anything you can tell me about yourself or what I may do for you?"

"To tell you, My Lady Morwen, I wish that I could," Carina replied. She said this so earnestly. It went to Morwen's heart and she thought much on it and of the look on Carina's face.

It was the day before Lady Morwen was to leave and she spoke with Malwell.

"Captain, my Captain," she smiled easily, "I do so hate to leave you and this lovely place. I do wish you might make me a gift of something here I treasure, to remember it by, perhaps?"

"Ask my Lady. Shall I give you a golden statue from the hall or another black pearl for your neck?"

"Yes, yes, a black pearl, but of a different sort. I ask for one of your servants. I should like to take her with me. None of mine do half so well, if I found favor with you?"

"Which one?"

"The little foreign one over there."

"Oh is that all?"

"Is that all? You should know yourself how quickly she picks up the language, and how competent she is, and through what she has struggled, all while doing such work as she is given."

"Of course, of course," Malwell answered. "They are all very happy here and I am sure it is only a joy to serve the Lady Morwen." He looked long into Morwen's face. He touched the pearl around her neck and smiled. "But I see something else in your eyes. This child is special to you. Is not that so, My Lovely Lady?"

"I cannot seem to hide anything from you, My Captain. I will confess. The truth is I remembered at last where I had first seen her. We crossed her path once. She was in a small boat out on the sea alone. Imagine that? I wanted to take her in then and would have, but the tether must have broken and she slipped away to her sorrow, I am sure, and mine as well. You see she would have been mine and perhaps was meant to be."

"Alone you say and what was the quality of her ship?"

"Of a most strange kind, a carved wooden thing with shapes of, oh, something and only large enough to hold one if that. It was her eyes I remembered, that bright sea green, and her hair streaming about her. She almost looked as if she had just come from the sea. I could not sleep last night, and I was looking through a book of history. I found a picture that looked so like the child. Suddenly I remembered it all."

"Really? How interesting, indeed, and so you would like her to come with you, and you see, I can't deny you anything that your heart of gold would wish. So take her then. Of course her aged mother is here, living in the Estate, and she goes to see her often; although she has probably not told you of that, because it saddens her to speak of it. She likes to pretend that her mother can still work. She is sickly, and perhaps it is only the hope of her daughter that keeps her going, but you need not concern yourself with that. Take, take, the child away," and he made a pretense of tears.

"Oh dear, I didn't know at all. Of course I shouldn't take her from her ailing mother. I imagined the child an orphan. I should have liked to care for her. But of course, no. I could not, now."

As his guests left him, Malwell returned to his study. His desk was overflowing with an odd assortment of books, papers, letters, and maps. To this he added the book Morwen had been reading, with a light toss. In it was a small likeness of the supposed Queen Adria. It fell open to this page. He made a wide sweep with his arm, scattering everything in his wake. He had decided upon one thing. Someone had slipped through his net, almost. He must tighten his grasp.

A Secret Mirth

It was strange how the rest of the day moved on as usual, only slightly more slowly. Lady Morwen and her company left with much fanfare. There were things to be seen to as the guests had gone. That night Carina was on her way, with the others, to go to her sleeping quarters, when Madame came and pulled her and Ara out of line, simply saying, still to Ara, "Your apartments are needed. You have a new room tonight. Follow the guard and go quietly." Then she quickly forced into Carina's hands a small bundle. It held Ancelin's basket, and a bit of bread.

They were led down the steps and out of the New Estate and across the river, blindfolded. After that it grew colder, and they were put on horses. It seemed they followed the guards through a winding wood, for the path was uneven and the trees whispered above. They traveled through the night and into the next day. They were put into boats. Carina's blindfold slipped just a little. They approached a large structure. As they grew closer, Carina could see that it was made of stone and they climbed large steps up from the water and finally crossed over a stone bridge. The whole time, she and Ara did not speak. Carina thought she should have been afraid and yet this new place, ruins though it seemed, gave her more of a sense of wholeness than did The New Estate, and so she followed on. At last the blindfolds were removed.

They made their way through a court and then up stairs and then down and down again. Carina could tell, even in the small light of the lantern and the faint light of the moon, that although the place was old, it was not in such bad condition. The walls seemed to be covered with carvings and mosaics, still intact and beautiful. It had been abandoned, but certainly not destroyed. What it needed was life again.

At last they reached a long corridor, from which many other hallways and doorways spread out. The guard stopped in front of one of the doors, turned the key, and motioned them in. They went in quietly and the second guard followed with a large metal lantern, with the pattern of stars cut through to give out light. Then he spoke to the younger guard, "Best go round now, check the locks, wouldn't want to be found wanting," and the guard looked around and moved back to the door.

Then the guard, still holding the lantern, and, with a hushed voice, addressed them saying, "I am a guard yes, but a friend too, and it is fortunate you have been assigned here."

The other guard returned, "The locks are as well as can be, until of course they're actually, well, locked." He stumbled over his words and looked around the room with a certain distrust.

"Time to go now, Delwin? I don't much like the looks of this place."

"Why yes, of course. I understand. It is a shame for the ladies." He winked at them as he said this and smiled. There was no real fear in his face, rather a secret mirth. Then he seemed to, absent mindedly, set the lantern upon an old table while looking for a key, which he then replaced in his pocket and, without picking up the light, he quietly walked out.

Carina and Ara were left with only the light of the lantern patterned with stars and with the moonshine coming in at chinks from the high windows in the far wall. Yet they felt not so very afraid, even when they heard the key turn and the door bolted, locking them in.

Moonlight Musings

Carina had to explain about Morwen and her guess that Malwell realized at last who she was. "Well that explains why we've been removed, but not why we've been placed here or even where here is," Ara spoke questioningly and then added, "Yet, perhaps, we can gather the clues and put something together. We know we crossed the river and we went a good bit through a wood."

"Then we crossed more water, but it seemed rather still."

"We also know what the guard said about us being fortunate, but pretending to be afraid like the other one."

"We must be at the old castle, Veradis Kel." They arrived at the conclusion together.

Ara mused, "Why did it take us this long to see?"

"It is sometimes easier to stay in the doubt, or the dark. It becomes a sort of pattern." Carina spoke quietly.

"Yes, but answers start as questions. One must begin somewhere. It may be in darkness, or in doubt, or in an aching longing. One must begin in dismay to go on to comfort."

"I suppose so. It is just such a shame to use this as prison. This is where a king should be, a real king."

"Yes, Carina, or a queen?"

Carina only shrugged. "I begged my parents, and even Altea, to bring me here. Many of the villagers only thought of it as a pile of unsafe or even haunted ruins. My father never minded that. He did not think much of a trip through the marshes, though, but he liked it better than the overland route. I think he was on the point of relenting when all this began. Altea only said, 'Your time to see the castle of old will come.' She was right. Here I am."

"Yes," Ara smiled. "But things will yet come right, and we are on our way. Now let's see what's here. We need to know as much as possible."

"If we only had a bit of moonlight, it would help," added Carina.

Then, as if in answer to her words, the clouds moved and the moon shone brightly through a series of high, small windows. They were merely slits from the outer wall, but grew larger at an angle through the thick stone walls, and so all along the room there were slants of moonlight, like stepping stones along the way. Ara smiled again, "You see. Elias hears you, even here."

Carina and Ara moved carefully along the walls. At first they found nothing very impressive. There were a few old chairs and a settee, near the fireplace. They were worn, but actually rather clean, and in the fire a few twigs were left and a stack of wood besides. In the darkness they had noticed none of this before. Soon, with the flame from the lantern they had a fire going, which seemed to help immensely to turn the cell into a room. Finally, at the farthest corner,

Carina noticed a fountain in a marble basin. It was white with blushes of pink, somewhat over grown with vines. It was also strangely clean and filled with clear water, and a small stream trickled from the fountain above.

After a drink, much refreshed, both girls returned to sit by the fire. Carina said at last, "I can't explain it, I feel as though my mother had been here, and I feel strangely safe."

Ara nodded in agreement, and the two fell asleep. They knew, at least, that they were not alone.

Later that night, both Ara and Carina woke suddenly to the sounds of thunder and the erratic light of the rain-filled skies. The fire had gone out. The farther part of the room had high walls, but was missing portions around a high window, and so the storm came in easily. In the farthermost corner they were dry against the walls, but cold. They pulled the settee across the room and sat facing one another, sharing Ara's cloak. She was never without it.

To Carina, Ara looked cold and small against the night, but bold even more so for it. It seemed the wind of the storm was there in the strength of her face and her resolve to endure it. With her back to the storm, she gave Carina some protection from the wind.

Finally, Ara spoke. "On nights like these, sometimes, I feel like I could fly. You have your river and seas, but I would take the skies if only..." Then she smiled and murmured, "My grandmother's cloak." Then added, "You know, she was one of the winged ones, and my mother had hoped that the wings not given to her, would appear in me. Instead, I have only these knots on my shoulders. Yet, this cloak of Grandmother's has served us well many years."

The storm continued and they tried to rest, in and out of sleep. Then Carina thought she saw a shape in the gathering darkness. She was not sure. It seemed to come closer. Then, he was there, standing behind Ara.

Elias stepped out of the darkness, with a dull light of his own, veiled by his cloak. He removed his hood and grew bright for an instant, far more than the lightning. He placed his hands on Ara's shoulders and spoke softly, "Ara, daughter, Eagle Maid, the time has come at last for you to take to the skies." Ara shuddered and turned, but he was gone. Then Carina was not sure whether she had dreamed it or not.

The rest of the night Ara writhed and turned. She could not sleep. At last exhaustion took over. Then, late in the morning, with the dropping of the last rains, Carina woke as a long, lovely wing fell across her face.

Ara thought she was dreaming. Then she remembered. "It was Elias. I thought, somehow, with your adventures, he only belonged to you. But see he has given me wings. He has called me, even me, daughter."

❧ First Flight

They quite forgot that they were hungry and weather worn. "Ara, you can fly? You can fly!" Ara stumbled as she stood up. The wings were not heavy but new to her sense of balance. She stretched one and then the other. She folded them and wrapped them around her. She ran her hands over the deep black of the outer edges, which turned silver, then white, then the brightest of blues.

"My grandmother," she murmured, "I remember again." She leapt into the air. The ceiling on the far end went up at least three stories, and she reached the top quickly and came down, if not gracefully, at least safely. Breathlessly she gasped, "It's amazing, so amazing."

When at last she was able to settle her thoughts she added, "I think those holes up there should be large enough for us to fit through and then, of course, we're free! I don't know where we'll go after that, but we can think once we're out."

Carina hesitantly added, "Are you sure you can manage flying and get me there too?"

"Well, perhaps if we had a rope, or my flying was much better, it would be easier, but still," and Ara's bright smile dimmed a little. "I did see my Grandmother do it. She carried my mother, once." She paused and then brightened a little, "And she used to carry me. We will certainly try."

But before they had a chance to begin in earnest, a strange new guard came in. Ara quickly hid her wings and tried to nonchalantly back into a corner. The guard took little notice of her. He looked at Carina, "Master wants no trouble from you. So in case you're gettin' any ideas...don't. I've been warned about you. Now come here. You're causing no mischief on my watch." He bound one of Carina's ankles to a chain attached to a heavy block. "No trouble," he repeated with a raspy laugh. Then a great gust of wind came through. He turned quickly and ran out.

Ara ran to her, "Carina, how awful. Does it hurt at all?" She began looking at Carina's ankle and the lock.

"No, not really. Only I was surprised, I suppose. Ara, if only he had waited a bit."

"We'll be just fine," Ara smiled as she tucked the tip of a wing under her cloak. "And I will be here to help you with anything you need."

Carina countered, "Oh no, Ara. If Elias gave you wings now, then it was for a reason now. We've checked the locks on the door before. Now I am chained. It may only grow worse. We can wait no longer. It is time for you to go, and you will find help. I know. You must be unseen, and if the guards return, I may be able to buy us time by pretending you are here asleep; and if it comes to it, he is most mad at me and not at you. Besides, we never know when someone may come. What if the guards returned and found you flying around the room? They surely would not leave you to it.

They may chain you as well or move us both. You must go for help, now." Then she paused and added softly, "I am the reason you are here in the first place, and I should like to know that at least you are free."

"Don't say that. I would just have been serving at his estate if I were not here. It isn't your fault and, if I had not been here, perhaps, I would have no wings at all."

"And now you do."

"But I'm not even sure where to start."

"I think it will come to you, Ara, Eagle Maid. This time I must stay behind."

Ara was still reluctant to leave. The thought that she could bring Carina help was at last the reason that made her go. So they parted, and Ara flew on her own over the old castle, the bay, and back up the River Blythe.

Carina, finding herself alone again, began to wonder what to do. She had simply to wait. But for how long? Then she remembered some words Elias had spoken, "Waiting doesn't diminish the hope, it enlarges it."

"It has certainly enlarged my hope for something to eat. I haven't even a crumb left. Ara didn't know."

"You have water," the voice came to her. She pulled herself along to the basin and found wrapped around it a bright green vine. On it grew glistening berries; they were hanging, ready to be picked. "Strange, I never noticed those before," she whispered.

Never Alone

C arina spent the next night restlessly. It was not only the sense of being alone, but the noise. There were scratchings and tappings and sometimes, she even thought, footsteps. She knew that it could be servants or soldiers, but why now and why always at night? There were stories of a strange being that inhabited the castle. She had never believed those, but now what was she to think?

Another day and night passed before the guards at last returned to her room. Delwin was amazed to find her so well and brought her a few loaves of bread and some apples, which he slipped though a hole in the door. She had made a pallet in the corner, which she hoped looked like Ara. The guards never even asked. They were distracted and impatient, and even Delwin did not enter the cell. "We're not to open the door, even. I'm sorry. My key for that has been taken." He spoke quickly, but kindly, "The others are afraid of this place. The Captain tells them lies of ghosts and strange accidents. He doesn't want them to come here. I don't know why he is so set against it, but he doesn't want people here anymore, and yet he won't just tear it down. Rather he has had some of the rooms put to rights and others used as storage. I know

204

little of that, what I do know is that this is a special room. You know your mother and I hid as many books as we could to keep them from being burned. They are in the chinks in the walls of this very room. I think there must be even more secrets to this place as well, and if you are brave, you can try to find them out. I hear the Captain even comes here himself and that perhaps it is really he who haunts this place now. There is certainly nothing worse than him here, I know. So you must be careful, but do not fear. Malwell fears his secrets escaping. He grasps so tightly. The others outside are restless. I shall tell them you had strange tales to tell, as I am sure you do. Please forgive that I cannot do more. Remember, he sometimes comes at night. Only, he will not come here. He is concerned with the grand rooms and those further up. He has been through these already and I've heard, for now, he only wants you well out of his way and safely kept. Alas, the only other gift. Your mother, I saw not even two days ago, and she is well. I don't know when I may be able to return, but if others are sent, I'm sure they will only leave food and go. So at least that is well. One last thing, be careful in eating the bread. Don't let it go long. Some of it's mighty hard already. I heard about your shackles," and again he smiled and was gone.

Why were people always leaving just when she wanted to ask a question? She thought over all that he had said. She puzzled at his last words too. As she took a bite of bread, she soon discovered the intent. The loaf held a small key. It was certainly not large enough for the bolted door. She looked at the chain on her ankle, with its smaller lock, perfect.

Carina had at first thought of all the books hidden around her and the supposed secrets of this place. She had never feared the old castle, even as a child. Altea had taught her so many wonderful things about Veradis Kel and those who once lived there. "Malwell has poisoned this too with his twistings," she thought. Well, if he should be upstairs looking for treasure, she would be downstairs finding it.

She began looking for the books. She looked for hours and hours and found nothing, nothing but rock and dirt, which stained her hands and scratched her fingers and turned them brittle from clawing at the damp stone. Still, there was nothing. She sat down in the gathering darkness and thought, perhaps he was wrong. This place is large. Perhaps, it was another room. Or, perhaps, he made it all up. Maybe it's just a trick. "Oh I want to believe him," she spoke aloud into the darkness. Then she remembered what else Delwin had said. If Malwell had been here first, perhaps they were gone already. Then why would he keep looking? No, it could not be. She simply must keep searching.

She fell asleep thinking of these things. She dreamed of a castle. It was a castle on a hill, old and grand with flags flying in the wind and perfume flowing from the flowers and gardens in its terraced walls and turreted towers. The gate opened for her, and she walked in. She followed a stream, and beside the stream, a small vine grew twisting its way along the river's path. She followed it. Then it began to grow smaller. Still she followed it. It ran through many rooms, up and down stairs, at last to a wall and there it seemed to stop. On the other side of the wall she could hear the water running through into a fountain.

She woke up thirsty. She stretched and went to drink. As she looked at the basin, slowly, a dim memory returned to her. She stared at the vines curled around it. These vines also sent out many shoots in strange patterns. Where the water overflowed, it followed the leaves and then trickled off in various directions, like little streams. Carina, with nothing better to do, followed the leaves and one of the streams of water until she came to a place in the wall where she could go no further. Then she began to dig. At first nothing happened, but then the stones grew loose. A few shifted and then, yes, there was a hollow. Inside this hollow two books sat!

She repeated the steps following each offshoot. She found so many wonderful volumes. Some were in strange languages. Others were old friends. She spent the rest of the day rapt in finding these words as long-craved company. She held them, smelled them, ran her fingers up and down their spines and over the pages. There were voices from many places and many times, all coming together in her mind and imagination. At last she found her own volume, neatly tucked away just on the other side of the fireplace. There was a fine chink that she would never have noticed without the leaves to guide her.

She thought she should have felt more relieved as she held the books, but then she realized that she had never really felt them as lost. They seemed to have a life of their own, something deeper than letters. She had had to search for them. She had them now and yet she craved them still. They were something both known and something mysterious, to be known. Yet, were they hers alone? She had trusted her own volume to the plan her mother and Delwin had concocted to save the books. It had been hard to let it go, but here it was.

Of course now she had them and could read them. But what else? She decided the best thing to do would be to take note of all the hidden places and then carefully put them back. She kept out her own, which she carefully tucked into the pocket in the back of her sash. Her long hair and the old shawl she had found did well to hide it.

The next morning she noticed a new shoot from the vine. It had grown quickly in the night and although it curled, it went actually over and into the hearth. The plant itself had become something of a friend, and without even thinking of it, she spoke aloud, "I've already found my books here, thank you just the same." But the vine, as vines will do, remained, looking green and knowing. So after a few hours of reading, she followed these last leaves into the hearth. It was much deeper than she had realized. She and Ara had only built a small fire on its edge. Now she could see that the vine actually reached deep into the wall where a little fire was smoldering and the leaves were beginning to burn. The glow sent out a strange scent of meadow flowers and at the same time gave a light that directed Carina far into the hearth, in fact to what appeared to be a door, covered with dust and ashes and time. She cleared away some of the dust. But there was, of necessity, a lock and no key.

She sat by the door, looking at the strange dark panels and realized that they were inlaid with etchings. There were symbols and pictures. It seemed to be a sort of story. There were even the winged ones, flying in a sort of dance. There was also an island. She looked at the keyhole and noticed its dark metal and intricate, jeweled design. Then she remembered the key Garna had given her, from those who had once served at Veradis Kel. She pulled it out from the hidden pocket within her sash and, with a trembling hand, tried it in the door. It opened easily, as if it too, suddenly, remembered.

The Stair Well

C arina followed the door into a small passageway. She had expected it to be a room like the one she had been in or a way out; still, she followed. The passage broadened slightly and soon turned into a narrow hallway, which, in turn, led to a flight of stairs. As she began up the stairs she noticed that they were not only steep, but slippery. Soon she realized the reason. There was a small trickle of water running down the steps. She looked again. Or, was it running up? Bidding her follow? She stepped in its path and finally came to a landing and another door. This time she did not hesitate with the key. The door slid open sideways, and she stood looking into yet another hallway. However, this one had many rooms on either side. She longed to look into them and paused, but the water ran over her feet and she walked on. Searching for its source, she went up another fight of stairs. These had windows on one side, giving her a view of the grounds, the towers, spires, hills, and cliffs of the island. The stairs, at last, came to an open air rotunda with pillars, sitting high on the castle. In the middle was something like a fountain, where the water came out, but it was deep like a well and seemed somehow to be taking in and overflowing all at once. Carina sat on the edge of one of the window seats, lining this fountain room, staring at this marvel. She was tired from the walk and ventured to bathe her face and hands in the water. It was clean and cold, and so she drank as well. It was abundantly refreshing. She wondered how there could be a spring so high and a well so deep, when she had just come from what seemed to be below it.

She turned to look around the space, and when her gaze returned to the water, there was a woman standing by the edge of the fountain. Carina had certainly not seen her there before. She was wispy, aged, and wrapped round with many layers of a fine cloth, shades of blue from that of the pale clouds to the deepest azure and all pure and waving as the waters. There was great patience in her eyes.

She smiled and spoke, "You are surprised, my child? You need not fear. I could do you little harm, if I wished, and certainly I do not wish it. The waters, however, are not to be trifled with. You have met them, and they are still; and you are still here. So I know all is well with you. Come, sit, and tell me your name. I am Anselwen, the Lady of the Castle Well."

"I am Carina and pleased to meet you, My Lady."

"And now where are you of?"

"I have lived in the village of Keldalee, and I have been locked in a room in this castle. Today I found my way to you, but I cannot yet readily say where I may be from."

"You answer well, like one who is still searching. Tell me of your travels," and so saying she produced, from Carina could not say where, a delicate tray set with tea and sweet rolls, dates and almonds, and golden pears.

So Carina related the story of her journey and Anselwen listened with much interest and patience. At last she spoke, "So you have come at last. I was told you would come. I did not know when, mind you. I have waited here, so long it seems, and yet I do not know. I have ceased to count in hours or days, and I have learned much from the waters. Yet your coming is to be a release."

"Release? May I ask from what?"

"I was bound to protect this place until the day of your coming."

"But how could you know I would come, when I did not know myself?"

"I beheld it a long way off, and so I have been waiting for you."

"But if you have protected all these things, and you are released, who will protect them now?"

"Those are deep questions better left for the well and not for me. I was told one would come. I have something, which now I will place in your hands."

From the folds of her garment, she produced a book, aged, but obviously cared for. She held it softly and looked at it. She smiled at Carina.

"I understand why I had to wait. There was a day when I would not have willingly given it...to anyone." Then she placed, with both hands, the book into Carina's hands, and they sat together.

At last Carina spoke, "The last of the three, in the language of the land. Yet one is missing, again. Now what I am to do?"

"I believe you must look to the well and listen to the voice of Elias. Did he not say you would never be alone?"

"Yes, how did you know?"

"For he has spoken the same to me, and I have found him true."

"Then we must continue on?"

"Yes, we must."

"But how?"

"Why I shall fly, I believe."

"And do you know a way out for me, perhaps?"

"You will fly too, but in a different manner."

"But you see I have no wings."

"Nor do I, now."

"Then you used to have wings, begging your pardon, My Lady?"

"Yes child, long ago. I was one of the winged ones. Only it is a long story, and my time here is almost at an end, I believe."

"But then how shall we fly?"

"You will see, my child."

Then Anselwen handed Carina a cloak of blue, light and waving.

"When you are ready, hold it well around you and glide unseen," she whispered this and then added, "And now we say farewell? My task here is finished, and I may go."

"Where will you go?"

"I shall dive at last into this well, deeper than I have ever been and see what becomes of me. You will stay, and see, will you not?"

"Yes, please."

Carina watched as Anselwen dove deep into the well, so far that she began to fear for her. But then she came up, smiling, not gasping, and stretched out of the well a most beautiful set of wings, yet somehow different from any Carina had yet seen. They had something of the movement of the waters in them. She looked stronger too, still wise, but younger somehow, except for her eyes. They held an ageless wisdom.

"Oh Carina I must embrace you once more and then be on my way. I have been given a great gift, and I must thank the giver." With that she kissed Carina upon her head and held her once more. "Remember, take care and glide unseen." Then she was gone and Carina was once again left alone. She looked over the edge of the tower. It was quite a long way down. Then she looked into the depths of the well. What she saw there one cannot quite describe to another, and yet after she had gazed, she turned. She took a firm hold of the cloak and jumped. It was not like falling. Nor was it quite flying either; she had seen others fly after all. She was gliding on the wind, lightly toward the ground.

 Unseen

W ithout a boat she was forced to swim the waters, which acted as a moat to the island castle. She really did not mind it. It felt good to be with the waters. Inside Ancelin's basket, the books stayed safe and dry, for she did not know the water would not harm them. When she came to the nearest bank, she stretched out in the sun and breezes to dry and rest and think.

Carina had now again two pieces of the book together. She must find the lost one, and it certainly would be no good to be captured again. Just then, she heard footsteps. She could see two of the guards coming toward her through the trees. She had no time to hide or to run. She jumped up and stood silently against a tree and held the cloak tightly along with her breath. The guards simply walked past her. She looked at the cloak, "Glide unseen," she murmured and added, "Thank you, My Lady Anselwen."

She followed the path, which they had come from. She rested in the forest for a few hours that night. By the next day, she crossed the river, by way of Malwell's new bridge, completely unseen, not that there were many to see her in any event. There were the guards and a few workers here and there. But there was no one in the market selling fruits or fish. There were few fishing boats, and it was all strangely quiet. The music of voices, of children playing, even of good hard work on the river; all these things were gone. This was no way for life to be lived. She had thought evil existed in other places only, but now it was here and it was strangely, horribly silent.

Carina, even though she did seem to be invisible, knew she still needed to be cautious. She could still be bumped into, she supposed, and if the veil fell from her, she would seem to suddenly appear. She walked into her village. The square was filled with dirt and a strange framework that looked like a building plan in progress or abandoned. It would be too difficult to manage a crossing through it. If her friends were those hiding in the forest her search could be endless. "If I could only overhear something," she thought, "I might at least have a chance."

She soon found herself on the road to the New Estate, although it was the last place she wanted to visit. She knew she must. There were a few workers about, and she waited until one was allowed in the gate and slipped in behind him. She followed him up the path and into the main hall, where another guard let him pass. He continued through the hall, but she went upstairs where she thought some of the others she had worked with might be cleaning. She passed a bedroom and noticed two women working. One seemed to be beating a rug, half hanging out of the window, but was rather listlessly going about her work. The other scrubbed the floor. At last, the one washing the floor paused and looked up and then around. Carina thought she recognized her face. It looked like Lilia. She had been kind to Carina, even when she was a stranger serving in the estate, and she had become a student of Altea's.

She turned to the other, looked around again, and then began scrubbing as she spoke softly, "He offered me a black pearl necklace."

"Who? Nuewell?"

"No. Captain Malwell."

"Is that why he called you yesterday up to the top floor?"

"Yes."

The other turned from the window and asked, "Why do you not wear it?"

"I told him I was flattered. Yet, it would be too great a gift for a servant when the fine Lady Morwen wears the same."

"What did he say?"

"He relented. He seemed flattered and pleased when I reminded him of Lady Morwen."

"But why not take one?"

"Do you know what they are?" Lilia countered.

"Jewels, precious jewels and you should not be so silly as to refuse one or his favor. I would not be so foolish if I were offered such a gift."

"Then it is a good thing you were not offered such. His favor is not a gift, nor are his pearls. They are dark mirrors, sponges, drains. He gives them as necklaces and as watches and medals and all for the sake of sickness. They can give illusions to the heart or pain to the body. They are no gift, but a curse. He even keeps one for himself to control the others."

"Oh and who told you that? Some silly old lady in the woods, one they say has wings? Really Lilia, grow up." Then she added, "Now get back to work or we'll hear it from Madame."

Carina stood lost in thought. Then an idea seemed to come to her as a wave lapping, the tide coming in.

Yes, she would go. Carina continued up the flights of stairs past rooms she had never seen. She passed guards, heavily armored, especially for indoor work, but they, of course, could not see her. At last she came to the rooms she thought she had intended, but not wanted, to find, Malwell's private apartments. Two guards stood on either side of the door. They were not the problem, exactly. If she opened the door, they would certainly notice. She quietly waited. She was nearly asleep on her feet, when at last the door began to rattle from within. As Malwell appeared the guards bowed, and Carina, in one mad dash, made it inside before they closed the door.

Breathless she stood, looking around, letting her eyes adjust. It was chilly in the room. The fire had died. The room she stood in seemed to be a parlor, lavishly furnished and decadent, with heavy red and black curtains and covers and couches and gold, so much gold, twisted, burnished into and over all of the fixtures. It was more than impressive. It was oppressive, and she moved on to look in another room. It was much the same, but with a bed. She shivered and crossed the parlor again and passed through two more, smaller rooms.

They were much the same, however. As she turned to leave the room she passed by a large curtain on the wall and ran her hand across it. It did not flutter and she realized it was somehow attached to the wall. She felt around its edges and then she hit upon a little spring just at the base. The curtain parted to reveal a dark door. She turned the handle and was surprised to find that it gave easily under her touch. It had been left unlocked.

She carefully stepped in and looked around. It was stuffy; the very air seemed heavy. There was still a great sense of opulence, but also of decay. There was a large desk, with a few papers, which still needed to be sealed, and wax and the signet were waiting. She noticed a map, but it was not of The New Estate, but of Veradis Kel. Some rooms were crossed through and others circled and others held strange symbols. Then she noticed another list. It read, "Relocated: Carina and Ara." Then she noticed at the bottom of the paper some scribblings. Out of them she deciphered the words, "Lady Adria, jewel, books, and Carina." Did Malwell know her secret? She had not time to think of that now. She searched for the book in every corner.

As she turned toward the last shelf, she noticed another curtain hanging in the corner. There was nothing particular about it except her desire to see what was behind it. As she pushed its weight aside, she found the entrance to a garret. Inside there was a high backed chair, with the back to her and, for a moment, she feared someone could be in it. As she stepped closer, she knew she was alone and yet not alone. In the chair was a large shell, half open and revealing a dark pearl, the size of an orange at least. It glowed, or rather oozed a sort of tainted dimness. As she drew closer she could see fleeting images appear and melt, but they were so vague and distorted she could make none of them out, nor did she want to. What she had first perceived as beauty, now made her feel sick and she knew the only thing to do was to get rid of the thing as quickly as she could. Yet, it held a strange kind of fascination. She feared its allure. She did not want to touch it.

She heard footsteps. She stopped and stood still against the wall to listen. The spring went and Malwell came in. Through the small slit between curtain and wall she watched, barely daring to breathe. He passed on the other side of the room and went to the desk. He sat down and hurriedly melted the wax and applied seals to several letters. Then he gathered them up and turned toward the garret. Carina almost gasped. He walked just past her. As he turned to leave, he seemed to look right through her. His gaze was cold and horrible, but cunning. Then she heard the turn of a key. This time he had remembered to lock the door.

Carina released a sigh. She slid to the floor and something caught her foot. She looked under the rug and felt along the floor boards, thinking on what she had heard Lieutenant Nuewell say. There it was; there was a trap door, behind a trap door. The spring gave and opened into a dark hole. She reached in and there at her finger tips, a box. She pulled it out and found it chained to something deep within the void and locked. Then she looked again. The lock had been tampered with. It looked secure, but, under a little pressure, it gave way. Again she thought of Nuewell, who knew so many secrets.

She opened the box and under several other papers she found her book. She grasped it and hugged it tightly.

Then again she saw the pearl, and now the thought came back to her. No. She would not touch it, but perhaps she could destroy it. She wrapped it in a large handkerchief and, holding the knot securely, but away from her own body, she turned to consider her escape.

Carina had only thought of getting in. She had not considered how she would get out. Then a breeze tugged from without on one of the curtains. It overlooked a roof garden on another wing of the estate. It was still rather high. But it was a window. She knew that the cape would work again and jumped into the wind. She glided easily down with much relief. She knew she must get to the river and quickly.

She did not go back through town, but through the woods to a strong stream that joined the larger river slightly higher up. At the water's edge, she stood with the pearl. She gazed at it, through the cloth. Her hands trembled. It seemed to call to her. She thought she saw the face of her father. She paused. Could it tell her what had become of him? No. Even if it could, her father would not want her to find out that way. She would follow his example instead. She built a small fire. Then she let the pearl go, even as her father had done. After a moment, it shattered and threw plumes of dark ash skyward. Then the stream swelled and washed the fragments away, fire and all. Finally it was done and taken in the current. Then Carina washed her hands as well. She was tired and suddenly so weary. She wandered farther into the woods and sat down at the foot of a great beech tree to rest. It seemed its roots cradled her and the branches in the breeze whispered above her head, even as dusk began to surround her.

She was suddenly startled from her rest when she heard a more hurried rustling of leaves. Someone was running toward her.

"Where can I go? Where can I go? He'll kill me if he finds me! I know he will. I know. Nuewell told him it was me. Why? Why would he do such a thing? Who would dare to disturb his apartments?"

It was Lilia. She was quite close to Carina now, speaking aloud although she was alone.

"He thinks I have taken the pearl. Madame warned me so. But how far can I run?" She went further into the woods and Carina followed. Soon the sound of horses reached them. Before they could be overtaken, Carina threw her cloak over Lilia and pushed a bundle into her arms. Then she spoke quickly, "Glide unseen. Take care. Find Altea. Now run!" When the guards caught up, it was Carina standing there.

Malwell dismounted his horse and called back the dogs. He strode over, and a flash of confusion mixed with disbelief flashed into his eyes. It quickly faded, into a new sort of intrigue.

"Well, well. What do we have here? A traitor, a pirate, a known felon? How far we have fallen," he spoke walking around Carina. "It appears to me to be a common criminal on the loose. My, but we are the clever one, for escaping and getting caught again, aren't we?"

"Bind her hands," he ordered the guards. Two dismounted and tied Carina's hands, and she was led back to the estate.

She was taken to a private courtyard, unbound, and given food and drink, which she left untouched on the table. She waited, and in time, Malwell entered, "Well, this is a surprise. Shall we be enemies or friends? I think your answers shall decide. Did you remove a certain article of importance from my possession?"

Carina sat quietly facing him.

He stood, "I say, girl, did you remove a certain item from my possession?"

Suddenly all of the fear she had felt, and expected to feel at such a moment, was overcome by something else; it was a strength not her own. She answered, "That depends on which article you mean? If you mean your sense of justice, your wits, or your compassion, I did not; although, they are clearly missing."

Malwell bit his lip and sighed deeply, trying to control his irritation.

"Did you take the pearl?"

"Yes."

Calmer now, "That's a good girl. Where has Lilia gone? How did she help you?"

"I do not know where she is. She had no part in helping me, and she wants no part of you."

His eyes flashed, "But how...and how did you come to find it, my dear."

"I glided unseen on the wind and landed here."

"Your words are nearly as twisted as mine."

"Not at all. I speak the truth as it is. You speak it as you wish it be. That makes a great difference."

"Hardly has it seemed to me. Now, simply tell me where it is, and this can all be quietly resolved."

"It is quite at home now."

"What do you mean? Where is it exactly?"

"I do not know. Many places, by now, I shouldn't wonder."

"Where did you hide it? Whom did you give it to?"

"It is not hidden. It was given and is free for the taking, if you gather the pieces, at the bottom of the river."

"Say you are lying and still it will be forgiven."

Carina was silent.

"You could not have, a thing of such power, such beauty, how…how…?" It seemed he really could not comprehend such an action. He paced for several minutes, and Carina stood.

"Well then, let us try something else. How did you manage to find your way out of the prison? Did you find something there that may be trivial enough to most, but of interest to great connoisseurs such as us? Perhaps you met someone who helped you? Perhaps you saw something interesting? Perhaps you, even now, have something you could give in exchange for the thing you have taken? Say it is so, and again, still all may be forgotten."

Again Carina was quiet.

"I know of your silly books. I know of your history. I even know of the said spring. If you have found something it would be wise to disclose it now."

Still, she was silent.

"Tell me what you know," his voice was low, firm.

"I could tell you many things, but I think it would do you little good. You do not understand the spring. It is not for the taking, but for the giving. There is one more thing you should know. I have seen Elias."

"Yes, I gather you have seen many people in your little cell. Perhaps you had tea with the queen there as well?" He answered coolly, but had given a little shutter at the mention of the name.

"As a matter of fact, I did see him in my cell. But that is not where I met him."

"Yes, and I suppose he is the one who freed you and let you get captured again. Toy on a string? You should imagine a better story for yourself, dear girl."

"I could not imagine a better one than what he tells. All that you seek, he is, and infinitely more."

"Really!" he sounded more vexed than ever. "Then perhaps you will not mind emptying your little sash, if you are as innocent as you seem to suggest?"

Carina untied her sash and turned the pocket inside out, showing it to be empty. He took it in his hands and held it upside down. Then he stared at her for some minutes as he walked around her again.

"Well, I see you are going to be difficult, and I had thought we might make up and dance as we once did. Do you remember? Did you tell your Elias of that? Oh what a shame, my pet. No matter now. We'll think of something else. Sleep well if you can, and perhaps in the morning we'll have another chat." So saying, he tossed the sash back at her and turned on his heel.

The secret pocket within the pocket had worked. She still had Garna's key and the books yet had a chance with Lilia. They were finally together and yet unseen. Did it matter if they were not in her hands?

Either Way

M alwell came the next morning out into the courtyard, where Carina had spent a chilly night, in an old chair under the walkway eaves.

"Oh, did you not like the accommodations? I am so sorry. You see we are rather full at the moment, with rather more important guests. Of course, if there was someone who could really prove that he or she was the one meant to rule, then this could all be ended. Of course, there is no one who could ever prove such a thing. It is all dreaming and superstition on the part of these people. They have chosen their ruler."

Then he turned to several of his guests who had just drift-ed out into the courtyard and he continued, "How can they say it is the truth, when no one can offer any proof? I offer them something real. Real trade, real riches, real living! That is why the people want me as their leader. I offer them something; something besides stories. Look where the stories have gotten them. If only they would hear and follow me, but some of them are a rebellious lot."

The guests who had been listening to this began to shake their heads.

"'Tis a shame, Captain, for sure," spoke the Lord Lucrue as he patted his wife's hand. "The Lady doesn't like to hear such troubling tidings." Then, to his wife he added, "Perhaps you should go inside my dear and rest a while. You have been up for nearly two hours now."

"It could go so well for them," continued the Lord Gaspert, smoothing his jacket and frills.

"Why do you suppose they are so hard headed?" asked Baron VonButiff.

But then one of the Misses Vaderhaults interrupted, "Who is that girl over there?"

"One of the servants gone astray, I shouldn't wonder," her sister answered, twirling a parasol around. "It is so hard to keep them in their place."

"No, no, kind ladies and sirs," Malwell interrupted, "This is surely an important lady. She is to be a queen."

"What nonsense is this?" demanded Lady Smudgitt as she stepped closer to examine Carina and then turned in disgust.

"Don't be hasty, my dear," spoke the Lieutenant. "Of course you are much superior in every way to this." Yet his speech trailed off as he looked at Carina.

They all did, for just a moment, and then Malwell recalled them.

"Well, at least that is what some say. The proof, however, is, as they say, in the pudding. She offers no proof, except for her conduct." He motioned to Carina. "She may seem quiet now and yet if you but knew. Why she has commandeered a royal ship for her own use and then ran it aground. She fired arrows at guards on an important official duty. She falsified her identify, lied to the Lady Morwen, who is no doubt still quite upset by the fiasco. She escaped from prison once already, she has spread the most horrible, vile stories, confusing the masses, and she daily leads those she calls friends into deeper danger and suffering. Would not you want her for your queen?"

"Oh, isn't there something that can be done?" asked the Lord Lucrue.

"For the girl here?" questioned Malwell.

"No, no, for my wife. She's fainted quite away. Call the servants." There followed a mild commotion as the Lady Lucrue was attended too.

"What, this girl? A common thief? A queen?" one of the Misses Vaderhaults stammered.

"Why, I never!" added the other.

"No, nor I," added another voice. They turned and on the arm of one of the guards Lethia came down into the courtyard. "Lethia?" murmured Carina.

She turned toward her escort who announced, "The Dame Lethia."

The gentlemen bowed. The ladies curtsied. Malwell smiled a twisted grin, "right on cue" he said under his breath.

"She's strange enough, but no. I can't say I see anything royal about her," continued Lethia. "I have had the displeasure of being some time at school with her; if you could call it a school. She has always been crude, and she has only grown worse, I see. Then, what do you expect from a poor little orphan, taken in by commoners?"

They went on taunting her, speaking of her parents, her past. She sank back into the corner. Then, suddenly, she stood up. They quieted. "This Captain has told but a half truth of my life, twisted, even as he is. I did commandeer a ship, to save my life, and I did fire on guards, after they first fired on me as I was alone on the river. I did take another name, because mine was not safe as you see. I do fear that I have led others into danger. But there would not be this danger if it were not for Malwell. Each chooses the path to follow. You say I am at fault because of my birth and my parents. What control have I on these? None. I could ask you what control have you of your behavior? I, at least, can be courteous. I would not treat someone as you have treated me and many others. You are all terribly rude, even to cruelty. I have loved and been loved. Can you say the same? Can you? Did you know also there are children stolen from their homes to labor in mines to find jewels to adorn your necks and collars? There are mothers made sick from the black pearls, given as gifts by Malwell? There are others, who have been slain, even, in protecting their own from Malwell's injustices? Yes, his men shot down my own father with arrows as he tried to protect my mother and the Eldress from further harm from Malwell's men." Then it seemed the tears caught in her eyes, and she took a long breath, daring them to disprove her truth.

They all quieted. Malwell shifted uneasily. The truth was uncomfortable.

"Lovely little speech. But you have no title. You have no right to rule," Lethia said calmly.

"Nor had you a title," Carina replied.

"Mine is an old family, and I am engaged to this guard, and for our service to the New Estate we are recognized as Knight and Dame." She held out a hand to show a ring. "So there," she added, and she stuck out her tongue.

Carina put her hand to her neck. She had given the jewel to Elias. She thought of the books. At least they were safe. "I have no tokens, now, to prove it, as you say. Yet, I do believe the word of Elias. I believe the truth of the Old Stories. I believe one such as this captain was never meant to rule. I believe there are many things that can be seen only without the eyes, and I do not expect you to understand this. I still do not myself. I believe there is truth, and Malwell does not speak it."

They looked around puzzled, gasping, sputtering, but unable to dispute.

"But are you the heir?" Malwell prompted and the others echoed.

"I have been told I am," she looked at Malwell, "by a source more reliable than you."

"You do not believe it yourself to be the truth?" asked Lieutenant Smudgitt.

"Truth is truth whether or not I believe it or whether or not I can prove it."

"My Lady," Malwell bowed as he spoke, "Had I but known. Of course anything you like, if you can but produce some tokens of this claim. If you cannot, you know what it means, of course?"

They mumbled among themselves, "imprison, expel, put her to work?"

"Oh no, I am afraid that, according to the laws of this land, written long ago, anyone who should lay claim to the title without producing the evidence of such, must be drowned in the river."

They were all rather quiet. Then Lethia broke the silence, "I believe drowning, for such a criminal, quite good actually."

"Shall we reconvene in three days time to test what this lady has said?" Malwell asked.

"I suppose we must," Lord Gaspert spoke, "as it seems she has made the claim."

The next morning, very early, Malwell came alone to see her.

"So you have not the jewel then? Did you give it away, silly girl that you are? Surely you did not misplace it? Or did you prefer the jewel that I gave you once?" Carina would not answer. "Then will you send for the other two pieces of the book?"

"You mean three don't you? You are always confusing the stories, aren't you?"

He glared at her and hurried inside. In the afternoon he returned. "You are rather pleased with yourself, aren't you, my girl? Well, it hardly matters. You cannot validate your claims. I may not have those books, but my stories are believed in spite of them. I may not have that jewel, but I have many others, which are coveted more dearly, and I still have one thing which I know Elias values. I have the missing heir to the throne. Checkmate, my dear. Well played, but no.

This one I win. It seemed he should be happy, and yet it was a terrible sort of face he made as he smiled.

He turned to retreat, and then he came back. "But how did you know of the hiding place of the book? It would not be easily found or taken, even for a scamp like you?" He seemed to ask this more to himself than to Carina. Then he looked at her. "Intelligence from inside? Will you give your sources?"

Still, Carina did not speak.

"I thought as much."

"Nuewell, come out here. I know you are there. You might at least make yourself useful. Now, Nuewell, make a careful search. Make a list of all those who might know best some such secrets. Oh, but that would include you, would it not?"

Carina interrupted, "You need not involve any others. I made my own plans. If I had any help from anyone here, it was purely coincidental. It is me you want to blame, is it not? Then blame me alone."

"Well, she speaks at last." Then turning to Nuewell he added, "It seems you've been spared by the courage of a common urchin. How does that feel? Perhaps that will be your best punishment, you fool. But I will be watching you, even more now." Then he turned and walked away slowly. "Checkmate, my dear. Checkmate still," he called out over his shoulder.

Nuewell looked at Carina, "I told you nothing."

"But you did know. I overheard you one day."

"Then, you have spared me when you could have done me harm? Why?"

"And why should I want to do you harm? You must not think as the Captain does. It is not the truth, or indeed the better way. But I believe even Lilia would forgive you and be glad for you to mend your ways."

This strange girl knew so much. Could she be right? He looked at Carina for a moment. Then he looked after the Captain. Then he looked at Carina once more, and he hurried away.

The next morning Malwell came again. "Well, it seems you have a guest. Although, I would hardly brag about it."

Elias walked in. Carina ran to him, and he held her for a moment. Then he looked at her and smiled.

"A moment," Elias commanded and the guards fell back.

"You have come. But you did not bring the books, surely?"

"No child. It is all safe, as are you. I have a request. It is very important. The next time you see me, whatever the state of things, that is when you must give me the books. Do you promise?"

"Yes, of course. Will you now tell them the truth?"

"Oh child, I have been telling them the truth. If only they would listen. Only, you must continue on and wait for me there, at Veradis Kel. I fear you will see me again, but then again still."

Malwell stood waiting, "I have other rather important guests," he called out.

"Then it is a shame they must waste their time waiting for you," Elias replied. Malwell stepped back and waited.

Elias stood with Carina and said a few more words of instruction and encouragement. Then he walked over to Malwell, and they began a discussion. Carina could not tell what it was about, except that at first Malwell looked scared, and then rather pleased.

Elias came back to Carina. "I have told Malwell that I am, indeed, The First Spring flowing from The Source. I am the one appointed to appoint the kings and queens and I choose whom I will, that is proof enough. I have taken up your claim, and so the law will be settled, and all made well."

"But how?" interrupted Carina, excitedly.

"You need not worry about how. Only remember your promise and think of your people. The prisoners are also to be released, but you must not trust him too well. You must head to Veradis Kel. There is help there. But you should not expect an easy time of it. Only, never think of yourself as alone, whatever it may seem. Now child, go in strength and in peace."

The Proof of Royalty

Carina was given a horse and then sent off into the forest. In a moment, she heard the rustling of wings, and suddenly, Ara and Ancelin were on either side of her. They both hugged her. Ancelin took the horse's reins, and Ara followed along beside her. "Elias told us to meet you here," she smiled. Together they carefully made their way to one of the hiding places, deep in the forest. There they cared for her, and Carina was also glad to see Lilia there. She was also glad to hold the books again and see all three of them. But how would it all come together? They were yet in pieces. Then she told Altea what Elias had said, and they talked over plans.

They had only one day of rest and mild feasting. Then a message came, brought on the wings of a bird, one of Altea's kind friends as she called them.

It read, "Caution. Plans. Changes in the ship. Rumors of release."

"What does it mean?" Lilia asked Altea.

"There is an old ship, moored, but it has acted as a secret prison as well. We heard that Malwell had plans to sink it, as a grand occasion of progress, without mentioning those inside."

236

"But who is inside, Altea?" Carina questioned.

"Does it matter? It may be a thief or it may be a friend. Either way, it must be stopped, and we have tried. Now we hear news at last that Malwell may release them. But why?" Carina thought she knew. Elias had done it. But there was also his warning.

The next day a message was circulated with Malwell's seal, saying that a great many prisoners were to be released, as a compliment to the "Lady Adria," and as a gesture of his supreme magnificence. However, they were subject to several small conditions, including obeying the new laws or choosing to go further upriver. A time was given when they were to be sent out into the square.

Altea organized those with her to meet them and direct them into the forest. They were divided into groups and led by various paths. They were to meet at Veradis Kel. There were many supplies there and what casts offs Malwell had been hoarding. With the key from Garna, there were no locked doors any longer. They hoped to get everyone there before Malwell caught up with them and tried to stop them. One party had gone upriver as a decoy already. For the rest, the forest provided much cover. Yet some were unwell and progress was slow.

The plans had been well made. Delwin had come and knew the best routes to take. Tobin had been released from downriver and Aidan appeared also. He said he had a message from a little bird and that Opal and Jasper were safe and well. Larsen, too, wanted to be of service, and he knew the way to the castle. With Altea, Ancelin, Carina, Ara, and Lilia, there were enough of them to each lead a group toward Veradis Kel.

They began their journey as some found family members and friends. There was a great strengthening joy in this. Yet, there was still much to be done, if they were to arrive safely.

They crossed the river. Those who could swim did. Many had to be taken by boat. They used any vessel they could find and still it was a long process. Guards and others still loyal to Malwell continued to watch and wait and poke fun at their leaving. Soon, however, they were across and headed into the bramble on the far shore. They continued to travel by night, the stars aiding the lanterns.

By evening of the next day, they were in sight of the castle. It seemed that this was what Malwell had been waiting for. He rode out of the thicket and announced to the crowd, "Ah dear citizens I was afraid of something like this. You've made a valiant effort, it is true. But let us be reasonable. Come back to the village and resume your work peacefully or, if not, you are free to go upriver, on my boat. You may not remain on this property, my property. If you attempt to stay here you forfeit your lives. I will make siege on my castle if I must. You are in violation of the conditions of your freedom and my soldiers are mounted and ready." With that, ranks of soldiers stepped out from the woods.

They continued on. As they did, Malwell's men sent a volley of arrows into the crowd. They began running for cover. However, Malwell did not know that Carina, too, possessed a key to the castle. Suddenly archers appeared on the castle wall. Malwell's men fired more arrows at these soldiers and at the people. Altea and the others hastened all those remaining outside into the fortress. They did what they could to defend themselves and their families and neighbors. Carina used a bow and Ara, Ancelin, and Aidan, flying, did the same. They also had their added weapons of wings as shields and in throwing off fine quills, rather like a porcupine. This is in fact what allowed Altea to get the last of her group through the woods and across the waters to the safety of the castle on the edge of the bay.

On the ground, Tobin and Delwin took up swords as did a number of the others who had once been guards. They were outnumbered, but they fought on. At last, everyone had made it to the castle as the cover of arrow fire flew from above.

On the other side, Tobin and Delwin barred the gates. Altea spoke, "Carina, I know you don't understand all, nor do I. However, the people must be led. There are many hurting, and there are those who can still defend. We must see to each." And so, in a kind of daze, they cared for the wounded and took them deeper into the castle. Then those who could still defend were armed and posted along the wall. As night approached, a new assault was made, and few were allowed to rest.

Carina made rounds to see the once prisoners who had been released, as Ara and Tobin did the same. She did not find her mother anywhere. She went to find Altea, who looked grave and was just coming to find her. "Child, I was afraid of such a thing. You know that we all placed our lives in danger, willingly, your parents included. I am not saying you should give up hope. You should never give up hope. But there is the possibility that Malwell, such as he is, did not set all of the prisoners free, thinking of such an event as this. There are others among us who have not been found."

"Altea, this is too much. I am not the one to rule all of this. I cannot be. I do not know what to do. When will Elias come?" She paused, "Do you think it safe to venture out?"

"There is a place on the western shore, a little cove. It is well protected by the castle and not to be reached except by way of the waters and then only in a small vessel. Will it do, my child?"

"Yes. Will you tell Ara where I am, and that she may follow, if she will?"

"Yes, my child. You need a friend."

Carina reached the cove. Altea was right. It was a quiet place. Ara followed a few steps behind her.

"Ara, Ara what is that in the water?" Carina began to run.

As they approached the shore, they saw something coming toward them, slowly on the surface of the waters. It came closer, and then it became clear. It was Elias, floating on his back, with a sword run through him.

Ara flew over him, and Carina waded out to him and then swam. The current was strangely slow. Carina pulled him closer to the shore until she could stand on the sand, and there she held him in the waters.

"Ara, how can it be?" Her words were not angry, but far away. Then more calmly she continued. "I made a promise, Ara. I made a promise to Elias that the next time I should see him, whatever the state of things, I would then give him the books."

"But surely, this cannot be so. How?" Ara spoke so gently, pleadingly.

"It must be so. Go, fly, and bring them. I will wait here." All the time she never took her eyes off of Elias. As Ara flew off, Carina stumbled back and then fell at the edge of the water. There she sat, and Elias washed into her arms. "Why?" she whispered over and over. "Why did you come here? Was it for the books? Was it for all of us? Was it for me?" Her only answer was the washing of gentle waves over them both.

When Ara returned with the books, she asked softly, "Carina, what shall we do with them?"

Carina looked at Elias and at the books. She took them and pierced them, ripping a hole in the binding and impaling them on the blade of the sword. Then she slipped them, one on top of the next, down over the blade and it held them in place as they lay on the chest of Elias. Then she placed Elias' hands over them. Finally, Carina wrapped her own cloak around him and kissed his hands holding the books.

All this time Ara had stood by, crying. She had gasped as Carina had cut the first book, but then she remained silent. When Carina had leaned back, Ara looked into his face and brushed a wing, softly around him. "Thank you. I did not get to say thank you." Then she turned away and pulled her wings around her.

"This," Carina said, "must be the proof of my royalty." She leaned over and touched his face again. How am I to let him go?"

"You've kept your promise. What else is there to do?" Ara said from behind her wings.

"I can't."

"You must let the waters take him, child." Altea's voice came from behind her. It was gentle, yet strong. "He is always our Elias. He is always who he is. He is always." Then the waters swirled around Carina. She let go. The waters received him and carried him on.

Carina stood and reached out to Altea. She hugged her and then she pulled away. For the first time, it seemed, Altea could not give her the comfort she sought. "Altea, it cannot be so. It cannot be as bad as that, and even if it is true, it is not the truth. Elias said I would not be alone. He told me to give him the books. He said all would be made well." Suddenly, she turned and ran. Ara started to follow, but Altea called her back. Together they walked in to tell the others. Meanwhile, Carina ran all of the flights of steps, slipping several times, to the room with the well. It was so quiet, so still. The water was not running. The well was a deep, unsearchable void.

She fell down beside it and watched her own tears fall over it. She gasped as she cried, pulling in quick, shallow breaths. Finally she dropped into an exhausted sleep. In the deep night, she heard a soft sound. It was like glass tinkling or rather water, and a small rivulet sprang up under her head. It rose into a fountain, and the water flowed around her and over her and through her, it seemed, filling the void. She watched it as it flowed out of the room and through the door over the steps. She stood. She would follow it. She would do as Elias would have her do, whether or not he was there before her. The waters still lived and so did she. She followed the water as it ran into a courtyard and filled a glittering pool, a tiled mosaic, and then it overflowed into a garden growing wild. The thirsty and hurting came to drink.

The following morning, just before dawn, Malwell made siege on the castle, with flaming arrows and trebuchets from across the water. The walls were damaged, but held. As night fell, the barrage stopped, but strange loud noises of deep drums, growling songs, and baying hounds were kept going.

By the next morning, a new fleet of ships could be seen in the bay. They were flying the flag of Lady Morwen, and her own *Blue Wasp* led them. They all supposed it to be reinforcements for Malwell. However, those aboard began to fire on Malwell's ships. They were driving his forces away from the castle and back to the shore and the river.

When there was at last a lull in the fighting, a messenger came from one of the ships. Morwen sent word to the castle that she had been informed of Malwell's dealings, by a reliable source, and was, for her part, very sorry and had sent a detachment of her own soldiers to be of help. Selwyn was to lead them and she was making haste with more help. She also returned a gift. Malwell had sent it to her, as a present, but she understood now to whom it belonged. Selwyn presented it to her, again. It was her own dagger, Fairlight. "I am sorry I could not come sooner My Lady, My Queen. The need for secrecy was great and the time was short. The Lady Morwen finally understood, after all. The pearl around her neck suddenly lost its luster a few days ago. After that she was ready to act." He paused, and then continued on, "I know you feel a great burden, but Elias did not set only you free or only the prisoners behind bars. Some cages cannot be seen. You must understand. We all owe much to him. He has given us each a great gift, My Queen."

"Thank you. You have done me a great service or rather a great many services."

"I would gladly do more, if I may?"

Carina smiled a little, "Yes, I would have you play. Play something that helps us remember Elias well before you return to the fight? Is there time for that?"

So Selwyn played and soon the main of the fighting was forced away from the castle, but still kept up. Selwyn returned to his ship and Ancelin and Ara flew out to see what was happening. The castle was no longer under siege, but more of Malwell's men had come from upriver. The battle was being waged in the bay and by the mouth of the river and even farther up. Carina kept reports coming in at the castle and arranged the archers on the wall to be ready at need. She also kept an eye on the currents, with Fairlight at her side.

The next morning Mawell sent word to Carina that he had a few special prisoners left, and if she valued those lives, she should surrender. He sent as a token her mother's silver ring, which had been etched by her father. Carina turned to Altea, "What must I do?"

Altea answered, "What would she want you to do?"

Carina thought she knew, but it was not the answer she wanted. Her mother would never have surrendered to one such as Malwell.

It was then that Ara came in, flushed with excitement and wonder. "I saw a small ship come into the western cove.

Larsen was aboard and helped to save his crew and bring them to safety. But what is more, Lilia saw something else, and this washed up beside us." She held out to Carina a book, large and curiously bound. Carina took it in her hands and opened it. "How can it be? It is my book, but not my book. It is all three of them, bound together again, beautiful, illuminated, whole and unfaded."

Carina announced that any who wished could come and see the book. For at least one part of it, many could read, and it was all lovely to behold. Then she returned word to Malwell that his terms were unacceptable.

The following morning, in the midst of heavy fighting, several prisoners appeared on shore. Malwell's great ship was poised at the opening of the bay, near the forested side and well away from the marshes. Carina had managed to leave the castle with the help of Anselwen's cloak. She could see her mother and several others, whose identities she could not discern. They were bound. They were about to be taken to the ship, and Carina was going to attempt a rescue, when the waters began to rise.

Then with the sound of many waters, a great wave rose up and standing in the wave was Elias, no longer dark and worn and bloody. He was whole and bright and healed. He stood on the waters. "My freedom is not conditional and I have set these people free. You shall not hold them back." He stood with his sword gleaming. He raised it in both hands, and then slowly pointed it directly at Malwell, standing on deck.

His face was stricken with fear and disbelief. The prisoners on the shore watched as the waters followed Elias' signal, and a great wave rose and gathered. Then Elias himself ran into the wave. The waters came crashing down on Malwell, washing him away and licking at the heels of his followers until they fled or were pulled into the waters.

The battle was washed away and Elias stood.

The Unfading

The last of the prisoners were finally free and beside her mother, wrapped in a faded and worn cloak, was another. He lay untied now, but in a huddled mass, barely moving. Carina ran toward him and uncovered the face of her father. In surprise, he gripped her face in his hands, "Can it be my own Carina? My Star, have they brought you here too?"

"Father. How can it be?"

Again he repeated, "Have they brought you here too?"

"No, father. You are free. We are all free. Elias has done it."

Ancelin rushed to him, but gave Carina a grave look and shook her head.

Calder lay on the ground, smiling up at Eldoris who was cradling his head and crying.

"All this time I thought you were far away and you were in that dungeon of a ship sitting right on shore. I would have broken in it if I had only known. I have waited so long to see you, and I thought I would be glad to die if only I could see your face once more. Now that it comes to it, I cannot bear to lose you again. My love, do not leave me. Please, don't go yet," she pleaded softly. "I could not bear another parting."

"My love," he spoke with a whisper, "I have thought of you every day and Carina. I could do little else. I thought much on every word you believed until I believed too."

Carina called for Elias. "You will help him?"

Elias looked at Calder, "Calder, my old friend. You stood up when few others would have, and you have held on so long. I think it is not your time yet to cross the Arvel Veil." And so saying he placed his hands on Calder's head, and the light returned to his eyes, and the strength began to flow to his body. He smiled up at Elias, "Thank you, My Lord."

"Calder, I have called you my friend," spoke Elias with a great smile, "Will you not again call me yours?"

"Gladly. Always. Elias, my friend," and Calder laughed as he had not in many long days.

In the following days the sick were cared for, and many who had lost homes were put into The Estate, trimmed down, and now called Adria's Palace. Work also continued on the old castle, Veradis Kel, and any needs were funded by Malwell's gold and Malwell's coffers.

Delwin and Tobin were among many who had been forced to work, but now delighted in being able to serve, and they too were to be knighted.

The book, now whole, was recovered as well and placed in the castle library, which Carina thought was nearly as grand as the one in Elias' house, only not so large. Altea was delighted to see that many of her books, which had been taken, were still whole and well. It was another reunion of old friends. Already they were working on making more copies.

There had also been a great celebration planned at the castle. The word had spread, and many guests were coming. From a balcony above a courtyard, Carina watched as they arrived. She saw her parents sitting together in a corner bower of wild roses. She saw Ancelin, wings spread and fluttering in the breeze, greet Aldwyn and then Altea came to greet him. Selwyn arrived, with his lute strung over his back and his sword at his side, and he smiled and bowed as he caught sight of Carina on the balcony.

Then she saw Keegan arrive with Garna and a toddling Ruby. Aidan appeared too with Opal and Jasper. Delwin came to help them in, and then Carina watched as Jasper broke away from the group and ran toward Ara and her father, yelling out their names. They were just under the shade of a trellis and talking. Aidan ran after Jasper. They turned, and it all happened so suddenly, the shock, surprise, doubt, certainty, and gratitude. The lost child at last was home and there was much rejoicing. The families seemed almost as one already, and Carina watched as Aidan took Ara's hand and bowed in greeting. Ara's wings were glorious. Aidan returned the greeting, and Ara's brother at last was home.

There was a dinner with such a table and food was taken to those who were unable to attend. Madame Pompadu even helped to serve, more graciously now. There was music and dancing too. Lady Morwen arrived, without her former retinue, and bowed to Carina. This time they were properly introduced.

Later, they all assembled in the great hall, and Elias spoke to them as friends. It is hard to recount exactly all he said, for although it was not a long story that he told, it seemed to rest in the heart of each as if being told only for that one. Perhaps you have felt something like it in reading an old book or hearing a song and knowing that the writer could not have known your thoughts and yet feeling as if he must know you, somehow.

Then Elias, standing before them, called to Carina. He placed the circlet that she had given to him around her neck, and placed the book in her hands. "You are heir to the throne of Kelwynden, forgotten, but not unmade. Some have waited long on this coming, but it is not the end. There are many who sacrificed to see this day and beheld it only as a hope. What great joy they have, and we join together in rejoicing with gratitude. Let us not forget. We tell the stories over and over again, and so we keep them alive. We share them freely. Now, Carina, the jewel and the book were the marks of the royal line of two houses joined, kept, and passed down. They were outward signs only. Now you have the heart needed as well. You shall at last know your first name, Amara, The Unfading, and now Ruler of Kelwynden, Queen of Veradis Kel, and Protectress of the Book of True Story." So saying he placed a simple crown upon her head, to much rejoicing.

Later in the evening Carina, alone, walked to look over the balcony out toward the waters. They lapped and danced on the shore. They even seemed to sing.

Elias found her there. "I must be going soon."

"I know," she replied softly without taking her eyes off of the sea.

"But I had hoped, my child, you might come and dance with me. Will you follow and let me lead?"

As she turned and took his hand she asked, "Elias, is this who I really am?"

He smiled, and his eyes took on a different sort of knowing brightness. "Oh, child, you are only just beginning to be. There is so much more to come."

Carina bowed, and her heart was full of joy.